THE NIGHTSHIFT BEFORE CHRISTMAS

BY
ANNIE O'NEIL

MILLS & BOON®

First published in Great Britain
By Mills & Boon, an imprint of HarperCollins Publishers
1 London Bridge Street, London, SE1 9GF

Large Print edition 2017

© 2016 Annie O'Neil

ISBN: 978-0-263-06698-2

Our policy is to use papers that are natural, renewable and recyclable products and made from wood grown in sustainable forests. The logging and manufacturing processes conform to the legal environmental regulations of the country of origin.

Printed and bound in Great Britain
by CPI Antony Rowe, Chippenham, Wiltshire

Christmas Eve Magic

Reunited on the night before Christmas!

The hospitals are bustling, the snow is falling and Christmas is fast approaching. Dr Emma Matthews and Dr Katie McGann have just one more nightshift to go, and for both the magic of Christmas is all around, because happy-ever-afters are about to land under their Christmas trees.

Let authors Annie O'Neil and Alison Roberts sweep you away on an unforgettable festive ride you won't forget in:

Their First Family Christmas
by Alison Roberts

and

The Nightshift Before Christmas
by Annie O'Neil

Available now!

Dear Reader,

Thank you so much for coming along to *The Nightshift Before Christmas*. I realise I have said this before—but this book really, *really* ate my heart alive when I was writing it. Josh and Katie were so real to me that my friends began to wonder if I actually knew them!

I don't want to give anything away at this point, but the loss they have each suffered is something I can imagine might too easily define a person. Grief is a strange beast, and it can shape-shift even the strongest of people into someone even they don't recognise themselves. Coming out of the fog of initial grief and back into 'the world of the living' is often overwhelming—especially if you don't have the one you love most by your side.

This is such a journey. One in which the gorgeous Josh and the heartbreakingly wonderful Katie are just trying so hard to *live* again—despite all that has happened to them. I hope you are as swept away as I was as they quest for their HEA in a busy mountainside hospital in Copper Canyon. And at *Christmas*! I do love a good holiday story, don't you? Just perfect for a little miracle of the L.O.V.E. variety.

Happy (Ever After) Holidays to you! And don't be shy about getting in touch. I can be reached at annie@annieoneilbooks.com or on Twitter @AnnieONeilBooks.

Annie O' Xx

Annie O'Neil spent most of her childhood with her leg draped over the family rocking chair and a book in her hand. Novels, baking and writing too much teenage angst poetry ate up most of her youth. Now Annie splits her time between corralling her husband into helping her with their cows, baking, reading, barrel racing (not really!) and spending some very happy hours at her computer, writing.

Books by Annie O'Neil

Mills & Boon Medical Romance

The Monticello Baby Miracles

One Night, Twin Consequences

The Surgeon's Christmas Wish
The Firefighter to Heal Her Heart
Doctor...to Duchess?
One Night...with Her Boss
London's Most Eligible Doctor

Visit the Author Profile page
at millsandboon.co.uk for more titles.

This one's for my guy.
You're my Christmas, birthday and HEA
all wrapped up into one handsome,
blue-eyed Scottish package.
Wifey xx

**Praise for
Annie O'Neil**

'This is a beautifully written story that will
pull you in from page one and keep you up
late and turning the pages.'

—*Goodreads* on
Doctor...to Duchess?

'A poignant and enjoyable romance that
held me spellbound from start to finish.
Annie O'Neil writes with plenty of humour,
sensitivity and heart, and she has penned a
compelling tale that will touch your heart and
make you smile as well as shed a tear or two.'

—*CataRomance* on
The Surgeon's Christmas Wish

'A terrific debut novel, and I am
counting down the days until the release
of Annie O'Neil's next medical romance!'

—*CataRomance* on
The Surgeon's Christmas Wish

**Annie O'Neil won the 2016 RoNA Rose Award
for her book *Doctor...to Duchess?***

CHAPTER ONE

"OKAY, PEOPLE! LISTEN UP, it's the start of silly season!"

"I thought that was Halloween?"

"Or every full moon!"

"First snowfall?"

"Hey, Doc? Is that where your locum tenens is? Stuck in one of the drifts?"

"He won't last long in Copper Canyon if that's the case. A man needs snow tires."

"A *woman* just needs common sense! I follow the snowplows! Got them tracked on my phone!"

Copper Canyon's Emergency Department filled with laughter. Impressive, considering they were down to a quality but skeleton staff. Never mind the fact it was almost always one of the busiest weeks of the year. The town was full of holiday visitors and the ski resort up the hill always had an emergency or six their small clinic couldn't handle.

Katie scanned the motley crew who would see her through Christmas Eve and, for some double-shifters, into the Big Day itself. Valley Hospital was no Boston General, and that was just the way Katie liked it. The facility was big enough to have all the fancy equipment, small enough to be able to give the personal touch to just about everyone who walked through those doors. And if they needed an extra hand, there were always the emergency services guys up on the mountain, willing to lend a hand. It wasn't home yet…but she'd get there.

"Thank you, peanut gallery. Time to focus." Katie tried her best to smile at the small but vital crew, all visibly buzzing with Christmas cheer. It wasn't their fault she wanted to rip every bauble, snowman and glittery snowflake from the walls. Someone else took that prize. "Thanks for wearing your red and green scrubs, by the way—you all look very…festive."

"Who doesn't love Christmas, Doc?" a tinsel-bedecked RN quipped.

Me.

"Right!" Katie soldiered on. They were used to her grumpy face—no need for Christmas to morph her into a jolly, stethoscope-wearing elf. "Just in time for the lunchtime rush, I've got our first Christmas mystery X-ray!"

A smattering of applause and cheers went up as

she worked her way through the dozen or so staff and slapped the X-ray up on the glowing board with a flourish.

"Any guesses?"

"Why would anyone stick one of those up their—?"

"I know! Especially at Christmas."

"At least it's not a turkey thermometer. We had one of those last year. Perforated the intestine!"

The group collectively sucked in a breath. *Ouch.*

"C'mon, Dr. McGann, that's too easy. Give us a hard one!"

"All right, then." She turned to face the cocky resident. "If it's so easy, what's your guess?"

"Cookie cutter?"

Katie winced and shook her head.

"Nope. Good guess, though. Try again."

She joined the staff in tipping their heads first in one direction then the other. It wasn't that tough...

"Tree decoration. Six-pointed snowflake. My Gramma Jam-Jam used to have one. It was my wife's favorite."

Katie's body went rigid with shock as the rest of the staff turned to see who the newcomer to the group was. She didn't need to turn around. She didn't need to imagine who or what Gramma

Jam-Jam's tree was like. She'd helped decorate a freshly cut fir in her old-fashioned living room as many times as she had fingers on a hand.

As her thumb moved to check that the most important finger was still bare, waves of emotion began to strike her entire body in near-physical blows. She willed her racing heart to still itself, but every sensory particle within her was responding to the one voice in the world that could morph her by turns into a wreck, a googly-eyed teen, a blushing bride…

Dr. Joshua West. Her ex-husband.

Well. He would be her ex if he would ever sign the blinking divorce papers!

She couldn't even manage to turn around and look at him, and yet her body was already on high alert to his presence. He was close. Too close.

She heard a shifting of feet. Maybe it was one of the nurses… Maybe it was… Her eyes closed for a moment.

Yup. There it was. That perfectly singular Josh scent. The man smelled of *sunshine*. What was *up* with that? It was the dead of winter. Freezing-cold, snowing-right-now *winter*. And yet she could smell warm sunny days and the rural lifestyle only her husband—her *ex-husband*!—could turn into something delicious. Talk about evocative! One whiff of that man had never failed to bring out her inner jungle cat. From all the excitement swing-dancing around her chest cavity in preparation for a high dive down to her...*nethergarden*...it was clear the cat had been in hibernation for some time.

Her spine did a little shimmy, as if she already didn't get the point.

She did a laser-fast mental scan of her medical books. Maybe her body was trying to tell her something different!

Frisson or *fear*?

Her tongue sneaked out and gave her lower lip a surreptitious lick.

Guess that answers that, then.

How could that rich voice of his still have a physical effect on her? Hadn't two years apart been enough to make her immune to the sweet thrill twirling along her insides every time she heard him whisper sweet—?

"Nice to see you, Katiebird."

Don't even start *to go there!* She took a decidedly large step away from Josh. *Sweet or not, they'd been* nothings *in the end.*

"Right, everybody! Let's get these patients better."

Katie clapped her hands together—more to prove

to herself that she had her back-to-work hat on than anything else. That, and she didn't want anybody around to witness the showdown she was certain was coming.

The group dispersed back to their posts, with a couple of interns still marveling over the human body's ability to deal with the unnatural. Precisely what Katie was experiencing at this exact moment. Fighting a natural instinct. Every time she laid eyes on Josh it was like receiving a healing salve. Her eyes were still glued to the X-ray, but she knew if she only turned her head she was just a blink away from perfection.

She sucked in a breath. Not anymore! No one and nothing was picture-perfect. Life had a cruel way of teaching that lesson.

"Are you ever going to turn around?"

His words tickled her ear again. The man clearly didn't believe in personal space when his wife was trying to divorce him.

"Are you going to tell me what you're doing here?" Katie wheeled round as she spoke. Her breath was all but sucked straight out of her as she met those slate-blue eyes she'd fallen so deeply in love with. It had been a long time since she'd last seen them up close and personal. A really long time.

She fought the sharp sting of tears as she gave a quick shake of her head and readjusted her pose. She could do nonchalant while her world was being rocked to its very core. She was a McGann, for goodness' sake! McGanns were cool, analytical, exacting. At least that was what she'd told herself when her parents had swanned off to another party in lieu of spending time with their only daughter. McGanns were the polar opposite of the West family. The Wests were unruly, wayward, irresponsible! Invigoratingly original, passionate, loyal...

Her teeth caught her lower lip and bit down hard as her brain began to realign the Josh in her head with the one standing in front of her. Thick, sandy-blond hair, still a bit wild on top and curling round his ears, softening the edges of his shirt collar. No tie. *Typical Josh.* He rarely did formal, but when he did...

She swallowed and flicked her eyes back up to his hair to miss out on the little V of chest she knew would be visible. No hat. *Natch.* Why follow the same advice you'd give your patients? There were a few flakes of snow begging to be ruffled out of the soft waves. Her fingers twitched. The number of times she had tucked a wayward strand back behind one of his ears and given in to the urge to drop completely out-of-character sultry kisses along his neck…

No! And double, triple, infinity no! No Josh West. Not anymore!

"Didn't the agency tell you?"

The expression on his face told her he knew damn well it hadn't told her. The twinkle in his eye told her he was enjoying watching the steam beginning to blow out of her ears. Typical. He always had been spectacular at winding her up and then bringing her to a whole other plane of happy—

Stop it, Katie McGann. You are not falling under his spell again.

"Tell me what?"

"No need to grind your teeth, darlin'." He tsked gently. "It'll give you a headache."

"Headache?" Maddening and headache-inducing didn't even *begin* to cover the effect he was having on her. "Try migraine."

"Good thing I'm around, then."

He gave her one of those slow-motion winks that had a naughty tendency to bring out the…the *naughty* in her.

"Those things can knock you out flat."

An image of a shirtless Josh slowly lowering himself onto her...into her...blinded Katie for an instant. The muscled arms, the tanned chest, slate eyes gone almost gray with desire and lips shifting into that lazy smile of his—the one that always brought her nerves down a notch when she needed a bit of reassurance.

She scrunched her eyes tight and when she opened them again there it was in full-blown 3-D. The smile that could light up an entire room.

"Josh, I can't do this right now. Our locum hasn't bothered to show, and as you can see—" her arms curled protectively around herself as the sliding doors opened to admit a young man with a child "—I'm busy. Working," she added, as if he didn't quite get the picture.

Never mind the fact he'd come top in the class above hers at med school, so clearly had brains to spare. Or the little part about how she was standing there in a lab coat in the middle of an ER. A bit of a dead giveaway. *Urgh!* If she used coarse language, a veritable stream of the colorful stuff would be pouring forth! Why was he just standing there? *Grinning?*

"What's the game here, Josh? Yuletide Torture?

Our last Christmas together wasn't horrific enough for you?"

His expression sobered in an instant. She'd overstepped the mark. There was no need to be cruel. They'd both borne their fair share of grief. Grinding it in deep wasn't necessary. They would feel the weight of their mutual loss in the very core of their hearts until they each stopped beating. Longer if such a thing was possible. Forgetting was impossible. Surviving was. But only just. Which was exactly why she needed him to leave. *Now.*

"Sorry, Kitty-Kat. You're stuck with me. I'm your locum tenens."

To explain why he was late for his first shift, Josh could have told Katie how his car had spun out on some black ice on the way in, despite it being a 4x4 he drove, and the all-weather tires he'd had put on especially, but from her widened eyes and set expression he could see she had enough information to deal with. The latest "Josh incident," as she liked to call his brushes with disaster, could be kept for another time.

"No. No, I'm sorry, Josh—that's not possible. We can't..."

He heard the catch in her voice and had to force himself to stay put. In his arms was where his wife belonged when she was hurting, but it was easy enough to see it was the last place she wanted to be.

He flexed his hands a few times to try and shake the urge. With Katie right there, so close he could smell her perfume… It would be futile, of course, but one thing people could always say about Josh West—he was a man who never had a problem with attempting the impossible. How else could he have won Katie McGann's heart? Cool East Coast ice princess falling in love with the son of a Tennessee ranch manager, scraping his way through med school with every scholarship and part-time job he could get his callused hands on? It was when he'd finally got his hands on her—man, they'd shaken the first time—he'd known the word "soulmates" wasn't a fiction.

"Dr. McGann?"

Both their heads turned at the nurse's call, and the strength it took to keep his expression neutral would have put a circus strongman out of work.

So. Katie had gone back to her maiden name.

Another nail in the coffin for his big plan, or just another one of Katie's ways of ignoring the fact they belonged together? That everything that had happened to them had been awful—but surviv-able. Even more so if they were together.

"Can you take this one? Arterial bleed to an index finger. He says it's been pumping for a while. Shannon's in with him now." The nurse held out a chart for her to read.

"Absolutely, Jorja. How long's a while?" Katie asked, taking the three strides to the central ER counter while scanning the chart, nodding at the extra information the charge nurse supplied her.

Josh took the chance to give his wife a handful of once-overs—and one more for good measure. It had been some time since his eyes had run up those long legs of hers. Too long. He'd been an idiot to leave it so long, but she had been good at playing hide-and-seek and he'd had his own drag-ons to slay. A small flash of inspiration had finally led him to Copper Canyon—the one place he'd left unexplored.

He stuffed his hands into the downy pockets of his old snowboarding coat, fingers curling in and out against the length of his palms. Laying his eyes on her for the first time in two years was hitting him hard. She'd changed. Not unrecognizably— but the young woman he'd fallen in love with had well and truly grown up. Still beautiful, but—he couldn't deny it—with a bit of an edge. Was this true Katie surfacing after the years they'd spent together? Or just another mask to deal with the disappointments and sorrows life had thrown at them in the early days of their marriage?

Gone was the preppy New England look. And in its stead… He didn't even know where to begin. Was this Idaho chic? Since when did *his* Katie wear knee-high biker boots, formfitting tartan skirts in dark purple and black with dark-as-the-night turtlenecks? Yeah, they would be practical in this wintry weather, but it was a far cry from the pastels and conservative clothes she'd favored back in Boston. The new look was *sexy*.

A hit of jealousy socked him in the solar plexus. She hadn't… He suddenly felt like a class-A *idiot* for not even considering the possibility. She hadn't moved on. Not his Katie. Had she…?

His eyes shot up the length of her legs to the plaid skirt and then up to her trim waistline, irritatingly hidden by the lab coat. His eyes jagged along her hands, seeking out her ring finger. Still bare. He would never forget the moment she'd ripped off her rings and slapped them onto the kitchen counter. Throwing had been far too melodramatic for his self-controlled wife. The word "Enough!" had rung in his ears for weeks afterward. Months.

He exhaled. Okay. The bare finger wasn't proof positive she wasn't seeing someone else, but it was something. He scraped a hand through his mess of a hairdo, wishing he'd taken a moment to pop into a barber's. But he hadn't worried a jot about what he'd looked like over the past two years, let alone worried about impressing another woman. From the moment he'd laid eyes on Katie to the moment she'd hightailed it out of his life—*their* life—he'd known there was only one woman in the world for him. And here she was—doing her pea-pickin' best to ignore him.

His eyes traveled up to her face as she scanned the chart, listening to the nurse. He knew that expression like the back of his hand. Intent, focused. Her brain would be spinning away behind those dark brown eyes of hers to come to the best solution—for both the patient and the hospital, but mostly the patient. One of the many traits he loved about her. Patients first. Politics later. Because there were *always* politics in a hospital. He knew that more than most. It was why staying at Boston General hadn't worked out so well. Why a new job in Paris just might be the ticket he needed to wade out of that sorry old pit of misery he'd been wallowing in.

But he wasn't going anywhere until he knew Katie was well and truly over him. He checked his watch. Seven days to find out if she was cold- or warm-blooded. It ended at the stroke of midnight on New Year's Eve. He'd either hand her a plane ticket or the divorce papers. He sucked in a fortifying breath of Katie's perfume. *Mmm...* Still sweeter than a barn full of new summer hay.

Well, then. He gave his chin a scrub and grinned. *Best get started.*

CHAPTER TWO

"WHAT YOU GOT THERE?" Josh stepped up to the desk, shrugging off his jacket as he approached. Out of the corner of her eye Katie could see Jorja's lips reshape into an O. Josh—or rather his body—had that effect on women. It was why she'd never thought she'd stood a chance. People always mistook her shyness for being stuck-up. But Josh had seen straight through the veneer and gone directly to her heart.

He turned his Southern drawl up a notch. He could do that, too. Pick and choose when to play the Southern gent or drop it if he saw it detracted from his incredibly sharp mind.

"Dr. McGann, may I help keep you out of the fray while you sort out the big picture?"

Katie eyed him warily for a second, then made a decision. By the hint of a smile that bloomed on his lips she could see it was the one he had been hoping for.

He would stay.

Never mind the fact that showing up on Christmas Eve when they were a doctor down wasn't giving her much of a choice. She had it in her to kick him the hell outta Dodge, if that was where he needed booting. But right now there were patients to see, and pragmatism always trumped personal.

"Twenty-five-year-old male presented with an arterial cut to the bone on his index finger." She tapped the chart with her own.

"Turkey?"

"Ham. Too easy for the likes of you."

She pressed the chart to her chest, claiming it as her own. Katie let her eyes travel along all six feet three inches of her ex. Josh had always been a trauma hotshot. And he'd always looked good. She'd steered clear of the Boston General gossip train, so didn't really know what path he'd chosen professionally after she'd left, but personally nothing had changed in the looks department. He still looked good. She looked away.

Too good.

"You're the next one down." She pulled the X-ray down from the lightboard and passed it to him with a smirk. "Make your Gramma Jam-Jam proud. You can put your stuff in my office for now—the staff lockers are further down the corridor and this patient's been waiting too long as it is."

She tipped her head toward a glassed-in cubicle a few yards away. Josh took advantage of the broken eye contact to soak in some more of the "New Katie" look. Her super-short, über-chic new haircut suited her. It sure made her look different. *Good* different, though. No longer the shy twenty-one-year-old he'd first spied devouring a stack of anatomy books in the university library, a thick chestnut braid shifting from shoulder to shoulder as she studied.

He cleared his throat. Whimsical trips down memory lane weren't helping.

"Green or red scrubs," she added, pointing to a room just beyond her office.

"You always liked me in blue."

The set of her jaw told him to button it.

"Green or red," she repeated firmly. "The patients like it. It's *Christmas*." She handed him the single-page chart with a leaden glare and turned to the nurse. "Jorja MacLeay, this is Dr. West, our locum tenens over the next few days. See that he's made welcome. His security pass should expire on the first of January."

"At the end of the day?" Jorja asked hopefully.

"The beginning. The very beginning," Katie replied decisively, before turning and calling out her patient's name.

He flashed a smile in the nurse's direction, lifted up his worn duffel bag to show her he was just going to unload it before getting to work. The smile he received in return showed him he had an ally. She shot a mischievous glance at his retreating wife and beckoned him toward the central desk.

"Don't mind her," Jorja stage-whispered. "A kitten, really. Just a grumpy kitten at Christmas." She shrugged off her boss's mysterious moodiness with a grin. "As long as she knows you've got your eye on the ball, she's cool."

Josh nodded and gave the counter an affirmative rap. "Got it. Cool. Calm. Collected. And Christmassy!" he finished with a cheesy grin.

"Says here you're double-shifting."

"You bet. Where else would a fellow want to see in Christmas morning?"

Jorja laughed. "Cookies are in the staff room down the hall if you need a sugar push to get you through the night. Canteen's shut and the vending company forgot to fill up the machines, so there might be a brawl over the final bag of chips come midnight!"

"Count me in! I love a good arm-wrestling session. Especially if the chips are the crinkly kind. I love those."

"I can guarantee you'll have a fun night…at least with most of us." She shot a furtive look down the corridor to ensure Katie was out of earshot and scrunched her face and shoulders up into a silent "oops" shrug when Josh raised his eyebrows in surprise.

"You two don't know each other or anything, do you?"

"We've met." It was all Josh would allow.

It was up to Katie if she wanted to flesh things out. He'd been the only crossover she'd allowed between personal and professional and he doubted she had changed in that department. She was one of the most private people he had ever met, and when news of what had happened to them had been all but Tannoyed across Boston General, it had been tough. Coal-pit-digging tough.

Jorja giggled nervously and flushed. "Sorry! Dr. McGann is great. We all love her. The ER always runs the smoothest when she's on shift."

Josh just smiled. His girl always strove to achieve the best and ended up ahead of the game at all turns. Except *that* night. She'd been blindsided. They both had.

He shook off the thought and waved his thanks to Jorja. First impressions? Young to be a charge nurse. Twenty-something, maybe. She struck him as a nurse who would stay the course. Not everyone who worked in Emergency did. She was young, enthusiastic. A nice girl if first impressions were anything to go by.

He'd gone with his gut when he'd met Katie. Made a silent vow she would be his wife one day. It had taken him a while, but he'd got there in the end. And today the vow still hit him as powerfully as the day they'd made good on a whim to elope. Five years, two months and fourteen days of wedded... He sighed. Even he couldn't stretch to "bliss." Not with the dice they'd been handed.

He thought of the divorce papers stuffed inside his duffel bag. There was only one way Katie could ever convince him to sign them. Prove beyond a shadow of a doubt that she felt absolutely nothing for him anymore. He gave a little victory air punch. So far he'd seen nothing to indicate she would be able to get him to scrawl his signature on those cursed papers tonight.

Just the shift of her shoulders when she'd heard

his voice had told him everything he needed to know. She could change her name, her hair and even her dress sense if she wanted to—but he knew in his soul that time hadn't changed how his wife felt about him. No matter how bad things had become. She couldn't hate without love. And when she'd finally turned round to face him there had been sparks in her eyes.

Katie stuffed her head into the stack of blankets and screamed. For all she was worth she screamed. And then she screamed some more. Silent, aching, wishing-you-could-hollow-yourself-out-it-hurt-so-bad screams. There was no point in painting a pretty picture in these precious moments alone.

Seeing Josh again was dredging up everything she had only just managed to squeeze a lid on. *Just.* In fact, that lid had probably still been a little bit open because, judging by the hot tears she discovered pouring down her face when she finally came up for air, she was going to have to face the fact there was never going to be a day when the loss of their baby didn't threaten to rip her in half.

What was he thinking? That he could saunter into her ER as if it were just any old hospital on any old day? With that slow, sweet smile of his melting hearts in its wake? She'd not missed the nurses trying to catch his eye. Jorja's giggles had trilled down the hallway after she'd stomped off. Josh did that to people. Brought out the laughter, the smiles, the flirtation. The Josh Effect, she'd always laughingly called it. Back when she'd laughed freely. Heaven knew, *she'd* fallen under his spell. Hook, line and sunk. If only she'd known how far into the depths of sorrow she'd fall when she lost her heart to him, she would have steered clear.

She swatted away her tears and sank to the floor of the supplies cupboard, using her thumbs to try and massage away the emotion. Her patient was going to be wondering where she was, so she was going to have to pull herself together. Shock didn't even begin to cover what she'd felt when Josh had walked into her ER. Love, pain, desire, hurt… those could kick things off pretty nicely.

"Of all the ERs in all the world, he had to walk into this one."

Talking to herself. That was a new one to add to her list of growing eccentricities. Maybe she should have fostered some of those friendships she'd left behind in Boston.

"Sounds like the start of a pretty good movie."

Josh's legs moved into her peripheral vision as his voice filled her ears.

"More like the end of one."

"No, that's the start of a beautiful friendship."

"Well—well…" She trailed off. Playing movie quotation combat with Josh was always a bad idea.

She huffed out a frustrated sigh. Couldn't she just get *a minute* alone? She should have gone to the roof. No one went there in the winter, and she relished the moments of quiet, the twinkle of Copper Canyon's Main Street. She swiped her hands across her cheeks again, wishing the motion could remove the crimson heat she felt burning in them. Against her better judgment she whirled on him and tried another retort.

"Should I have said 'of all the *stalkers* in all the world'?"

"Oh, so going to the supplies cupboard to track down some mandated holiday scrubs has turned me into a stalker, has it?" he asked good-naturedly.

The five-year-old in her wanted to say yes and throw a good old-fashioned tantrum. The jumping-up-and-down kind. The pounding-of-the-fists kind. The *Why me? Why you?* kind. The Katie who'd shored up enough strength to finally call their marriage to a halt knew better. Knew it would only give Josh the fuel he wanted to add to a fire she could never put out.

She wasn't going to give him the satisfaction of knowing how much she still cared. That had been his problem all along. Too trusting that everything would be all right when time and time again the world had shown him the opposite was true. Who else had become an adrenaline junkie after their daughter had been stillborn? Hadn't he known how dangerous everything he'd been doing was? And she'd always been the one who'd had to pick up the pieces, apply the bandages, ice the black eyes, realign the broken nose... Trying her best to laugh it off like he did when all she'd wanted to do was curl up in a corner and weep.

Couldn't he see she had to play it safe? That losing their daughter had scared her to her very marrow? If she were *ever* to feel brave enough to move forward—let alone try and conceive again— he needed to call off his game of tug-of-war with mortality.

She scratched her nails along the undersides of her legs before standing up, using the pain to distract herself from doing what she really wanted.

"Large or extra-large?" she bit out.

"Guess that depends on if you need me to play

Santa later." He grabbed a pillow from a shelf and stuck it up his shirt.

Without bothering to examine the results, Katie yanked a pair of extra-large scrubs from a nearby shelf. Not because she needed a Santa but because she didn't need to see how well he filled out the scrubs. The first time they'd met—*woof!* And she was no dog owner.

The first time they'd met... He said it had been in the library, but she was convinced to this day that he'd made it up. The day she'd first seen him—easily standing out in a crowd of junior residents, all kitted out in a set of formfitting scrubs—his eyes had alighted on her as if he'd just gained one-on-one access to the Mona Lisa herself... Mmm... That moment would be imprinted on her mind forever... She'd never let anyone get under her skin—but she'd been powerless to resist when it had come to Josh.

"Green! Good to see you remember red always makes my complexion look a bit blotchy."

Katie blew a raspberry at him. She wasn't playing.

"Or is it that you remember green always brings out the blue in my eyes?" He winked and took hold of the scrubs, trapping her hand beneath his.

Just feeling his touch reawakened things in Katie she had hoped she'd long-ago laid to rest. Her eyes lifted to meet his. Stormy sea-gray right now. Later… He was right. Later they'd be blue, and later still the color of flint. She had loved looking into his eyes, never knowing what to expect, trying to figure out how to describe the kaleidoscope of blues and grays, ever-shifting…ever true.

As the energy between them grew taut, the butterflies that had long lain dormant in her belly took flight, leaving heated tendrils in their wake. She tugged her hand free of his and gave him a curt smile. Physical contact with Josh was going to have to be verboten if she was going to keep it together for the next eight days. It was bad enough he'd seen her red-rimmed eyes.

She glanced at her watch.

T-minus…oh, about one hundred and ninety-two hours and counting!

"Twenty-four hours."

"Beg pardon?" Josh shook his head.

Hadn't he been riding the same train of thought she had? If she'd gone off on a magical journey down memory lane, the chances were relatively high he'd done the same thing. Different tracks— different destinations.

She cleared her throat. There was about half an ounce of resolve left within her and she needed to use it. "I'm giving you twenty-four hours."

He raised his eyebrows and gave her his *What gives?* face.

"Oh, don't play the fool, Josh. You've ambushed me. Pure and simple. And on—" She stopped, only just missing having her voice break. "It's the minimum notice I have to give the agency if I want a replacement."

"What are you on about, Kitty-Kat?" He pulled himself up to his full height. Josh always played fair and he could see straight through her. This was a below-the-belt move.

She jigged a nothing-to-do-with-me shrug out of her shoulders, her eyes anywhere but on his. "If it's quiet enough we might be able to let you go earlier without telling the agency."

She might not want him here, but she didn't want to tarnish his record. He was a good doctor. Just a lousy husband. She squirmed under his intent gaze, pretty sure he was reading her mind. A sort of, kind of lousy husband.

"Don't be ridiculous. Christmas is always busy! You're going to need me. What kind of man would

I be, leaving you to deal with a busy ER all on your own?"

"That's terribly chivalrous of you, Josh. I'm going to need a doctor—yes. But I don't need *you*." She looked at her watch again, not wanting to see how deep her words had hit. Laceration by language was *way* out of her comfort zone—but tough. Josh had pushed her there—and she had an ER to run.

"Sorry, I've got to get to this patient."

"Yup! I'm certainly looking forward to mine!" He mimed snapping on a pair of gloves with a guess-it's-time-to-suck-it-up smile.

If she was feeling generous, she had to give it to him for keeping his cool. Assigning him a rectal examination as a "welcome gift" was not, she suspected, the reunion he had been hoping for. Then again, finding out her estranged husband would be her locum for the next week wasn't much of a Christmas present for her, so tough again! Hadn't two years' worth of sending him divorce papers given him enough of a clue?

"Uh... Kate?"

"Yes?"

"Are you going to move so I can get my patient's Christmas ornament back on the tree?"

"Yes!" she blurted, embarrassed to realize she'd been staring. "Yes, of course. I was just…" She stopped. She wasn't "just" anything. She stepped back and let him pass.

"I'm happy to see you, too, Katiebird," he said at the doorway, complete with one of those looks she knew could see straight through to her soul.

She rubbed her arms to force the accompanying goose bumps away.

"Me, too," she whispered into the empty room. "Me, too."

"Hello, there… Mr. Kingston? I understand you've got a bleeding—" Katie swiftly moved her eyes from the chart to the patient, instantly regretting that she'd wasted valuable time away from her patient.

Unable to resist the gore factor, the young man had lowered his hand below his heart and tugged off the temporary tourniquet the nurse had put in place. Blood was spurting everywhere. If he hadn't looked so pale she would have told him off, but Ben Kingston looked like he was about to—

Oops!

Without a moment to spare Katie lurched forward, just managing to catch him in a hug before he slithered to the floor.

"Can I get a hand in here? We've got a fainter!"

Katie was only just managing to hold him on the exam table and smiled in thanks at the quick arrival of— Oh. It was Josh. *Natch.*

He quickly assessed the situation, wordlessly helping Katie shift the patient back onto the exam table, checking his airways were clear, loosening the young man's buttoned-at-the-top shirt collar and loosening his snug belt buckle by a much-needed notch or two as she focused on stanching the flow of blood with a thick stack of sterile gauze.

"Got a couple extra pillows for foot elevation?"

"Yup." Katie pointed to the locker where they stored extra blankets and pillows. "Would you mind handing me a digital tourniquet first? I'll see if I can stem the bleeding properly while he's still out."

"Sure thing." Josh stood for a moment, gloved hands held out from his body as they would be in surgery, and ran his eyes around the room to hunt down supplies.

"Sorry, they're in the third drawer down—

Wait!" Her eyes widened and dropped to Josh's gloved hands. "Weren't you in the middle of...?"

She felt a sharp jag of anger well up in her. *Typical, Josh!* Running to the rescue without thinking for a single moment about protocol! Was simple adherence to safe hygiene practices too much to ask?

"Done and dusted." He nodded at the adjacent exam area. "He's going through the paperwork with Jorja." He took in her tightened lips and furrowed eyebrows and began to laugh. Waving his hands in the air, still laughing, he continued, "You didn't think...? Katie West—"

"It's McGann," she corrected quietly.

"Yeah, whatever." The smile and laughter instantly fell away. "I always double-glove during internal exams. These are perfectly clean. You should know me better than that." His eyes shifted away from hers to the patient, the disappointment in his voice easy to detect. "You good here?"

She nodded, ashamed of the conclusion she'd leaped to. Josh was a good doctor. Through and through. It was the one thing she'd never doubted about him. He had a natural bedside manner. An ability to read a situation in an instant. Instinctual. All the things she wasn't.

She slipped the ringed tourniquet onto the young man's finger and checked his pulse again. It wasn't strong, but he'd be all right with a bit of a rest and a finger no longer squirting an unhealthy portion of his ten pints of blood everywhere. He'd need a shot of lidocaine with epinephrine before she could properly sort it out, so she would need to wait for him to come to. Being halfway through an injection wasn't the time when a patient should regain consciousness. Especially when Josh was leaping through curtained cubicles, coming to her rescue. She jiggled her shoulders up and down. It wouldn't happen again.

"Are you nervous, Doc?"

"Ah! You're back with us!" Katie turned around in time to stop the young man from pushing himself up to a seated position. "Why don't you just lie back for a while, okay? I have a feeling your finger didn't start bleeding half an hour ago, like it says in your chart, Ben."

He looked at her curiously.

"Is it okay if I call you Ben?"

"You can call me what you like as long as you stitch me up and get me outta here, Doc! It's Christmas Eve. I've got places to go…things to do—"

"Someone to drive you home?" Katie interrupted. "After your fainting spell, I don't think it's a good idea for you to get behind a wheel."

"And I don't think it's a good idea for *you* to boss someone around on Christmas Eve!"

Katie backed away from Ben as his voice rose and busied herself with getting the prep tray ready. Emotions ran high on days like this. Especially if the patient had had one too many cups of "cheer." Unusual to encounter one on the day shift, but it took all kinds.

"Cheer" morphed into cantankerous pretty quickly, and Ben definitely had a case of that going on. She stared at the curtain separating her from her colleagues, knowing she'd be better off if there was someone else in the room when she put in the stitches.

She sucked in a breath and pulled the curtain away. "Can I get a hand in here?" She dived back into the cubicle before she could see who was coming. Josh or no Josh, she needed to keep her head down and get the work done.

"Everything all right, Dr. McGann?"

At the sound of Jorja's voice, Katie felt an unexpected twist of disappointment. It wasn't like she'd been hoping it would be Josh. Her throat tightened. *Oh, no...* Of all the baked beans in Boston Harbor... Had she? *Clear your throat. Paste on a smile.*

"Yes, great. Thank you, Jorja. Nothing serious, just thought we could do with an extra pair of hands now that Mr. Kingston here has rejoined us."

Josh tried his best to focus on the intern's voice as he talked him through how he saw things panning out on Christmas Eve based on absolutely zero experience, but he couldn't. All he could hear was Katie, talking her patient and the nurse through the procedure in that clear voice she had. The patient had definitely enjoyed a bit of Christmas punch before he'd arrived, and Josh didn't trust him not to start throwing a few if he was too far gone.

"Hey." He interrupted the intern. "What did you say your name was again?"

"Michael," the young doctor replied, unable to keep the dismay from his face. He'd been on a roll.

Tough. Fictional projections weren't going to help what was actually happening.

"Michael, what's your policy on patients who've had a few too many?" He mimed tossing back some shots.

"Oh—each ER head is different, but Katie usually calls the police." He looked around the ER as if expecting to see someone stagger by. "Why?"

"Just curious." He gave Michael's shoulder a friendly clap with his hand, hoping it would bring an end to the conversation. "Thanks for all the tips," he added, which did the trick.

He tuned his hearing back into the voices behind the curtain where Katie was working. The patient was young and obviously a gym buff. As strong and feisty as she was, Katie was no match for a drunk twenty-something hell-bent on getting more eggnog down his throat. Drunk drivers on icy roads were the last thing the people of Copper Canyon needed on Christmas Eve. Or any night, for that matter.

"Okay, Ben, you ready? I'm just going to inject a bit of numbing agent into your finger."

"What *is* that?"

Josh inched a bit closer to the curtain at the sound of the raised voice.

"It's a small dose of lidocaine with epinephrine," Katie explained. "It will numb—"

"Oh, no, you don't!" The patient—Ben, that was it—raised his voice up a notch. "I've been on the internet and that stuff makes your fingers fall off. No *way* are you putting that poison in me!"

Josh only just managed to stop an eye roll. Self-diagnosis was a growing epidemic in the ER…one that was sometimes harder to control than any actual injury.

"I think if you read all of the article you'd find that's more myth than reality."

Always sensible. That was his girl!

Ben's voice shot up another decibel. "Are you telling me I'm a *liar*?"

"No, I'm saying digital gangrene is about the last thing that's going to happen if I—"

"You—are—not—putting—that—sh—"

"Hello, ladies." Josh yanked the curtain aside, unable to stay quiet. "Need an extra pair of hands?"

"No," Katie muttered.

"Yes," Jorja replied loudly over her boss.

"They're trying to give me gangrene!"

"Really? Fantastic." Josh rocked back on his heels and grinned, rubbing his hands together in anticipation. "I haven't seen a good case of gangrene in ages." He flashed his smile directly at Katie. "Are you trying to turn Mr. Kingston here into *The Gangrene who stole Christmas*?"

Everyone in the cubicle stared at him for a moment in silence.

"The Grinch!" Josh filled in the silence. "Get it? Gangrene? Grinch?"

There was a collective headshake, which Josh waved off. "You guys are hopeless. They're both green!"

Jorja groaned as the bad joke finally clicked.

"Well," he conceded, "one's a bit more black and smelly, and isn't around for the big Christmassy finish, but, Ben, my friend…" Josh took another step into the cubicle, clapping a hand on the young man's shoulder from behind and lowering himself so that he spoke slowly and directly into the young man's ear. "I've known this doctor for a very long time, and if she needs to stabilize the neuronal membrane in your finger by inhibiting the ionic fluxes required for the instigation and conduction of nerve impulses in order to stem the geyser of blood shooting from that finger of yours, she knows what she's talking about, hear?"

Ben nodded dumbly.

"Right!" Josh raised a hand to reveal a set of car keys dangling from his fingers.

He saw Katie's eyebrow quirk upward. He would have laid a fiver on the fact she was thinking he'd taken up pickpocketing to add a bit more adrenaline to his life. He'd win the bet and she'd be wrong. He'd just seen enough drunks in his Big City ER Tour. The one where he had done everything but successfully forget the brown-eyed beauty standing right in front of him.

He cleared his throat and stepped away from Ben. "You owe Dr. We—Dr. McGann an apology. And while you do that—" he jangled the keys from his finger "—I'll just be popping these babies over to Security until we get someone to pick you up."

Ben opened his mouth to object, his eyes moving from physician to nurse and back to Josh before he muttered something about being out of order, his mother's stupid car, and then, with a sag of the shoulders, he finally started digging a cell phone out of his pocket.

"Excellent!" Josh tossed the keys up in the air, caught them with a flourish, gave Jorja a wink and tugged the curtain shut behind him before anyone could say *boo*.

"Well…" Josh heard Jorja say before he headed off. "He's certainly a breath of fresh air!"

Katie muttered something he couldn't quite make out. Probably just as well.

Josh grinned, his shoes glued to the floor until he was sure peace reigned behind Curtain Three. He heard Katie clear her throat and put on her bright voice—the one she used when she was irritated with him.

"Now, then, Ben, if you can just show me that finger of yours, we can get you stitched up and home before you know it. Jorja? Could you hand me some of the hemostatic dressing, please? We need to get the wound to clot."

Josh began to whistle "Silent Night" as he cheerily worked his way back toward the main desk. Job. Done.

"How long do you intend to continue this White Knight thing?"

Josh's instinct was to smile and tell her he would wield his lance and shield as long as it took for her to see sense and come back to him. Longer. Until the day he died, he would protect Katie. He'd taken a vow and had meant it. He had broken part of it, and he was going to spend the rest of his life making good on it. Even if that meant walking away, no matter how hard it hurt.

But this was work. Personal would have to wait.

"Where I come from, people stick around to help one another when the going gets tough." He laid the Tennessee drawl on as thick as molasses. It always got to her and this time was no different.

He watched as her hands flew to her hips in indignation, then shifted fluidly into a protective, faux-nonchalant crossing of the arms. Her eyes widened, the lids quickly dropping into a recovery position. One of her eyebrows arched just a fraction before her face became neutral again. But she couldn't keep the flush of emotions from pinking up her cheeks.

He shifted his stance, ratcheted his satisfaction down a couple of notches. He wasn't playing fair. He knew more than anyone that teamwork in an emergency department was something Katie valued above all else. Unless, it seemed, it came from him.

He stood solidly as she gave him the Katie once-over. He wouldn't have minded taking his own slow-motion scan over the woman he'd dreamed about holding each and every night since she'd told him in no uncertain terms she'd had enough of his daredevil ways. He'd have to play it careful. Divorce rules shifted from state to state, and he hadn't checked out Idaho. If she'd moved to Texas he would have shown up a lot earlier. No need to wait for a signature there. As it was, he thought two years had given them each more than enough time to know they were meant for each other. Given *him* enough lessons to know she'd been right. He'd suffered enough loss to know it was time to change. Move forward—whatever shape that took.

"Where are you staying?"

Unexpected.

"Here." He pointed at the hospital floor.

There went that eyebrow again.

"Locum tenens wages aren't enough to get you a condo?"

He shook his head. "I didn't know how long I'd be staying."

She refused to take the bait.

"Usually housing comes with the contract."

What *was* she? The contract police? Or... A lightbulb went off... Was she trying to figure out where he'd be laying his sleepy head? Was she missing being held in his arms as much as he had longed to hold her? Truth was, he never bothered with separate housing on these gigs. Hospital bunks suited him fine... Friends' sofas sufficed when he was back in Boston. Home was Katie, and it had been two long years...

He heard the impatient tap of her foot. Fine... he'd play along.

ANNIE O'NEIL

49

"Not this time of year. And it was too short a contract for me to put up a fight."

Katie's jaw tightened before she shifted her chin upward in acknowledgment of the obvious. She knew what he meant. The locals had dibs on all the affordable properties. Everything went to the top one hundred highest-paid, most famous, with the biggest bank account, et cetera, et cetera. Life in Copper Canyon was a heady mix of the haves and those who *worked* for the haves.

Mountain views, private access to the slopes, sunset, sunrise, heated pools, wet bars, ten thousand square feet minimum of whatever a person could desire—you name it, they had it. Copper Canyon saw most of America's glitterati at some point, on the slopes or at one of the resorts…if, that was, they didn't have a private pad.

"You staying at your parents'? I remember them having a pretty plush pad out here and not using it all that much."

Risky question, but he couldn't imagine why else she would have moved here. She walked over to the board and began erasing patient names and re-arranging a few others.

"They're usually at the Boston brownstone or in the Cayman Islands, right?"

"Jorja? Could you make sure the tablets are all updated to reflect what's on the board? We've got quite a few changes to note," Katie called over her shoulder to the main desk.

"Sure thing, Dr. McGann. On it!"

Josh leaned against the wall, one foot crossed over the other, hands stuffed in his pockets, happy to just watch her play out her ignoring game. He threw in an off-key "Rudolph the Red-Nosed Reindeer" whistle for good measure.

"And let's pop something different on the music front, Jorja. Some *nice* carols."

Josh grinned at Jorja, dropped her a wink and dropped his whistle simultaneously.

"They just don't stop, do they? Your parents?"

Only the squeak of the whiteboard pen could be heard over the usual hospital murmur.

Wow. Having a conversation with a brick wall would have yielded more return.

"The indefatigable McGanns! That's how I always thought of them."

Katie's lips tightened. She didn't do chitchat. Especially when it came to her parents. They were the source of any well-packed baggage Katie had hauled around through the years. Parents who'd discovered they hadn't really been up to parenting so had handed it over to nannies and boarding schools to do the work for them. They were harmless enough folk at a cocktail party, but he knew their lack of interest as parents hurt Katie deeply.

"I'm not staying there this week."

Interesting.

"I always stay at the hospital over Christmas," she volunteered hastily, with a quick pursing of her lips. "My parents have come in to ski for the week—"

Josh snorted and was relieved to see Katie join in with an involuntary snigger.

"Well…at least they'll look fabulous in their ski gear before they hit the cocktail circuit."

Her eyes flicked away with a shake of her head. She must have remembered she'd told herself not to enjoy being with him.

"It's easier not to get stuck in a storm if I'm here."

Wow! Two whole sentences! They were on a roll. He kept his ground. Nodded. Tried not to look too interested. He'd learned long ago that it took a lot to get Katie talking, but once you opened the floodgates…

"So…where are you really staying?"

Bang goes that theory.

"Honestly, Kit-Kat. My plan was to just stay here."

Her brown eyes were briefly cloaked by a studied blink. Then another. Her lips twitched forward for a microsecond in a moue. Was that a response to his being there? Had an image of the two of them wrapped together as they'd always been in bed flashed across her mind's eye as it had his?

He cleared his throat and shifted his stance. "Casual" was getting tough to pull off. What he wouldn't give to take the two steps separating them and start to kiss those ruby lips of hers as if each of their lives depended on it. It felt as though his did, and standing still was beginning to test his fortitude.

"I see." She abruptly turned to face the main desk, where Jorja was checking in a new patient. "We'd best get you to work, then."

Fair enough. *She wasn't saying no.*

And... A smile began to tug at the corners of his mouth. Depending on how you looked at it, Katie was saying *yes*. Yes to his staying. Yes to his being in the hospital. Yes to their being together.

Okay, it was a bit of a leap, but he was willing to take the risk. In for a penny and all that...

He pushed away from the wall and took a step

behind her when she turned back to face the board, unsurprised to see her shoulders stiffen…then relax when he kept just enough space between them for her to know he wouldn't do what he'd always done before their lives had been ripped in two.

He closed his eyes and pictured the scene. She'd be studying something—anything—an X-ray, a chart, the wall—it didn't matter. He'd step right up behind her, arms slipping round her waist, hands clasped against her belly, his chin coming to a rest on her pillow of chestnut hair or slipping down alongside her cheek for a little illicit nuzzle or to drop a kiss on her neck…

He heard her sigh at the exact same time he was blowing out a long, slow breath between his lips. *Oh, yeah.* They were on the same page all right. It just hadn't been turned for a while.

"Hey, you two—you're in for the Secret Santa, right?"

Josh and Katie both whirled round to see a grinning Jorja holding out a Santa hat with folded pieces of paper being rapidly jiggled around.

"Count me in." Josh reached into the hat and grabbed a bit of paper. If he was going to show Katie he knew how to settle down, enjoy small-town life… "Who doesn't love a bit of Secret Santa action?" He turned to Katie. "That is if it's all right with the boss lady?"

"Who am I to curtail your holiday cheer and our small-town ways?"

And they were back in the ring! Three years ago the idea of going back to his small-town roots would have made him run for the hills…or the bright lights of Manhattan, more like it. But after he'd quit Boston for Manhattan, Chicago, Miami, none of them had stuck. Not one had sung to him. Nothing worked without Katie.

"I'm just a small-town boy, and nothing says home like…" His eyes sought hers and in that instant he was sure each of them knew what he might say.

"Like what, Dr. West?" Jorja pressed.

Katie. It had always and only been Katie.

"Like having an opportunity to put down roots! In the form of a Secret Santa. I just love a good old-fashioned round of Secret Santa."

Too emphatic?

He felt Katie giving him a curious glance. *Good.* He wanted her to see the changes. Maybe not all of them. The pins in his leg could wait. And the scars along his hip and spine. It wasn't looking like she'd be ripping off his clothes for a moment of unchecked ardor anytime soon, so he was good with that. But he'd been careful that she didn't see him walk too much. She'd know. She'd definitely know. And she'd never come back to him then.

"Dr. McGann? Are you taking part in the draw?"

Jorja waggled the hat in front of his wife's face. She might be a good nurse, but that girl sure didn't read body language all that well.

He watched Katie put on her bright face and return her focus to Jorja. "Of course. In for a penny..."

Josh felt Katie's eyes land on him as the words came out of her mouth, her hand plunging into the hat blindly to grab a bit of crumpled paper.

She remembered. They'd both said it. A lot. Especially in the early days of their marriage, when they'd needed every penny to repay their medical-school bills, making their own way after just about the best elopement a couple could ever have had when Katie had decided her parents didn't deserve to put on a society wedding. A church full of her parents' business associates and bridge pals mixing with his ruckus of a family, who would show up to a black-tie event wearing their funeral clothes? No, thanks.

His lips twitched as her eyes stayed locked on

his. They'd spent just a few hundred dollars on rings, the honeymoon, and a huge chocolate cream pie that they'd set between them at a roadside diner and eaten in one go… Then, not too long after, they had been putting down deposits on cribs and—

Josh raked a hand through his hair and looked away first. It was still hard to go there. Still impossible to believe they'd really lost their little girl. That sweet little baby who'd never even had one chance to look into her parents' eyes…

"Right! You said you wanted me to get to work." He craned his neck to look around at the waiting room and stuffed the bit of paper into his lab coat pocket. "Who's next?"

Katie had to shake her head for a minute before she could think clearly. Having Josh here was like receiving a physical assault of emotions she hadn't wanted to feel again.

Pain…

She unnecessarily scrubbed her hands through her super-short hair, having forgotten, just as her eyes connected with Josh's, that she didn't have a ponytail to curl her fingers through anymore. *Yup.* The pain she could certainly do without.

Fear.

That Josh would be safe. That he'd come home from his latest escapade unscathed. That he would come home at all. Bearing another loss in the wake of their stillborn baby girl...wondering if he'd well and truly be there for her if they decided to try and conceive again... No. She just hadn't been able to do it.

Desire.

The desire felt good. *Too* good. And it was too much of a link to the pain and the fear. A trilogy of Josh, all wrapped up in a gorgeous sandy-haired, blue-eyed package she had never been able to resist. But she had to. For her sanity, first and foremost. For her heart.

"What do you think? You happy to let me go with the photocopy girl?"

"Beg your pardon?" Katie forced herself to focus on the words coming out of Josh's mouth about a patient newly arrived from an office party gone wrong. Photocopies. Bottoms. Broken glass.

His front tooth was still crooked. She'd always liked that. The imperfection made him more... perfect. Hmm... Maybe she shouldn't focus on his mouth. His eyes—definitely blue-gray in this light. Flinty? Steel-blue. Was there such a thing? And with little crinkles round the edges. Those were new. Sun, maybe? Or just the passage of the two years they'd put between them?

It might have felt like an eternity, but two years wasn't really that long. Then again, they'd been through a lot. But Josh had always seemed impervious to it all. Definitely a glass half-full— That was it! *Glasses.* He probably just needed glasses. Typical Josh to put practical needs like getting his eyes checked on hold. She tilted her head to the side. They *were* kind of sexy. The crinkles…

Nope. *Nope.* Still not hearing words. Still not focusing. What about the little bridge between his eyes? That was just like anyone else's. Just part of someone's face. A plain old face just like any other doctor in any other hospital. With a nose and high cheekbones and two perfectly formed… *Argh, no!* And she was back to his lips.

"Apologies, Dr. West." She put on her best interested face. "I didn't quite catch that."

A low laugh rumbled from his chest. Josh knew damn well she'd been ogling him and he was loving it. From the first day he'd draped a stethoscope round her neck, he'd known he had the power to cut straight through her prim-and-proper exterior and bring out the hidden tigress in her. The one she hadn't known existed. Bookish only children who preferred the company of their elderly nannies weren't obvious contenders for being horny minxes aching to see how it felt to be scooped up in a single swoop, her legs wrapped round his waist, his hands cupped on her—

"...derriere."

"Beg pardon! What was that again?"

This time Josh didn't even bother going for subtle.

"Katie, do you just wanna sneak off and make out for old times' sake while the anesthetic gets to work?"

"What? *No!*" She shook her head, sending a horrified look over her shoulder to see if anyone had overheard him. "No!" she added, with a look. She didn't *make out* with people. Let alone with the one man on the planet she needed statewide clearance from if her brain was ever going to work properly again.

She forced herself to play a quick game of catch-up.

"You say she broke her office's copy machine by sitting on it? Why on earth was she doing *that*?"

"You never butt-copied—?" Josh stopped himself, his smile shifting from astounded to tender. "It's something that happens when an office party gets out of hand. This gal clearly likes to get her cray-cray on."

"I have *no* idea what crayfish have to do with it."

"Crazy!" Josh laughed. "Cray-cray is crazy, if you're down with the kids—know what I mean?" He struck a pose for added emphasis.

Katie sniffed. She could do zany. If she put her mind to it. But photocopying her butt? That was just ridiculous. The germs on one of those things should be off-putting enough!

"Well, you two sound perfect for each other."

Katie saw the sting of hurt her words caused and wished she could yank them straight back. Josh might do wild but he also did wonderful. If only he hadn't kept pushing the boundaries after their loss. If only he'd convinced her he could play things safe—even for a while—they might…

"I best get on, then."

Katie watched as Josh turned and made his way toward the curtained cubicle where his patient was waiting. There was something…different about his gait. Something different about *him*. He'd changed. Really changed. Her teeth caught hold of her lip and gave it a contemplative scrape.

Changed enough to hear what she had to say?

A series of loud guffaws burst from the curtained area where Josh was de-sharding his patient's booty.

No. Same ol' Josh! Some stray Christmas spirit must have sneaked into her coffee that morning. No one changed *that* much. She would just see through the time they had to work together as professionally as she could. No point in reopening old wounds. She'd borne enough hurt for a lifetime.

She scanned the board and picked a good old-fashioned broken arm. Some enthusiastic decorative touches to a snowy rooftop, no doubt. Fixing. Setting. Repairing. That was what she did. It was how she survived.

Once again she shook on her bright smile and pulled open the curtain.

"Right! Mr. Dawsen, I understand you've broken your arm?"

CHAPTER THREE

"I'LL JUST BE in the residents' room—cool?" Josh popped a finished chart onto the RNs' central desk, flashing a smile to the two nurses trying to untangle a set of twinkling lights. A patient's or some late decorating? They paid him no attention, so he hightailed it down the corridor, hoping for a few moments to regroup. It was time to pull up his socks and tell Katie the truth. The real reason he was there.

She'd yanked six of his safety-net days out from under him, unwittingly putting all his partridges in the one pear tree. It was do-or-die day *now*. For a man who didn't plan much, he had definitely planned this out. A whole week to gauge her mood…time to maybe inject a bit of romance into snatched moments alone. But with this stupid twenty-four-hour thing she showed no sign of shifting from, he had to get a move on. They were just a few hours away from midnight, and once that clock pinged upon the Christmas star, his time

ANNIE O'NEIL   63

would be well and truly running out. Josherella
was going to have to get a move on.

He looked at his backpack, slung on the back of
the lone chair parked across from the bunk he'd
thrown himself on for a catnap. He wouldn't have
been surprised if the sheaf of official papers lurk-
ing in the side pocket had taken on a life of their
own, unzipped the bag and come out and danced
at him like an evil sugarplum fairy...or whoever
the evil one was in *The Nutcracker.*

He cursed silently. He'd once loved Christmas
and all the schmaltzy, cheesy, sentimental stuff that
went along with it. When they'd lost their daughter
just a few days before the holiday, it had sucked
the season dry of any good feeling. He wanted
that back—and the only way to get it was to woo
his wife back into his arms. And if this was the
season for miracles he was a first-rate candidate.

Otherwise...? Otherwise he would have taken
the job in Paris when he'd got the offer. Moved to
France to study with the most elite team of mini-
mally invasive fetoscopic surgeons? Hell, yeah! It
would have been a gargantuan leap forward for his
career. He'd spent the past two years doing locum
residencies in every single obstetrics unit he could.
He would never know why his little girl had been

stillborn—but if he could help other women he'd be there.

But his heart wouldn't be. And to end up in the City of Love without the woman he adored by his side would have been pointless. Not to mention the fact that Dr. Cheval insisted on total focus. No distractions and no demons. Right now Josh was hauling those things around big-time.

When the job offer had come, he'd seen it as life's way of grabbing him by the scruff of the neck, giving him a right old shake and demanding, for once, that he take responsibility for everything he had done. Own up to how his behavior had driven his wife away. And after she'd gone he'd pushed at life a bit more. A *lot* more. Life had pushed back, and now he had the metal infrastructure to prove he hadn't come out the winner.

He gave his head a good old scratch, shooting a look up to the heavens to see if there were any clues there.

Mistletoe.

Of course. *Love.* The high-voltage current he'd felt the first, second and every other time he'd laid eyes on his wife was electric. But going to the city where hand-holding and kisses on bridges and feeding each other delectable morsels of...

Hey! Now, *there* was an idea. He and Katie had always enjoyed a good picnic. Out on the common—or on a bench if it was pouring down—regardless of the sideways glances they'd received from passersby. It was what supersized umbrellas were made for, right?

A smile lit up his face. He'd do a Christmas dinner picnic! The smile faded just as fast. The canteen was closed. The way the snow was coming down meant leaving the hospital would be a challenge. Or just plain stupid. He'd already done stupid...

"Hey, Dr. West." Jorja poked her head round the corner with an apologetic expression. "Sorry to ruin your break, but we've got mass casualties coming in!"

Adrenaline shot through him and he was up and out of the bunk before Jorja had even removed herself from the door frame.

"What happened? How many? Do we have enough on staff? Is there any chance of diverting any of the patients to another hospital?"

Jorja's eyes widened, along with her mouth. Streaks of red began to color her cheeks.

"Uh..." She pushed at the floor with the stub of her toe.

66 THE NIGHTSHIFT BEFORE CHRISTMAS

"Sorry, too much television! I forget Copper Canyon is totally different from what you get out east."

"There are two. Patients, that is. With gastro. Dr. McGann is already down there."

Josh's heartbeat decelerated and he tried not to laugh. Much. The poor girl looked mortified. He slung an arm around her shoulders and tugged her in for a half hug as they made their way out into the main corridor. "Hey, Jorja, don't you worry. I can adjust my big-city ways…"

The words stopped coming. What the heck was he doing, bragging about his big-city machismo when he'd grown up in a town with two unlit junctions? Junctions where he'd been guaranteed to see his math teacher or his father heading off to the cattle markets. There was no hiding anywhere in that place if you stuck around—which was why he'd loved losing himself in the big city. And then he'd met Katie…like an angel he hadn't known he'd needed to meet. Found him. That was what she'd done. She had found him. Shown him how important it was to be grounded.

He looked straight up, silently cursing the invisible heavens. She was his lighthouse, his beacon, his…whatever analogy best fit the scene. She was his heart. His soul. And if he didn't get a move on he was going to lose her for good.

"Uh… Dr. West? Are you trying to…?" Jorja was shifting underneath his arm, turning toward him, shifting her gaze upward as well.

Damn. Mistletoe.

Katie heard them, then saw them. A twist of nausea squirled around her stomach as she took in the nervous laughter, the awkward shuffle of feet and the chins tipping up toward the ceiling. Jorja had practically covered the hospital in mistletoe, so it was hardly surprising that the one person who would find a way to put it to use was Josh. He had always been a flirt. It was his nature. To charm, to delight, to dazzle.

She turned away quickly, not wanting either of them to see the hurt in her eyes, the sheen of tears she'd only just managed to check when she'd spotted them. The last thing she was going to do was stick around and watch her husband kiss someone he'd only just met!

At least she knew Josh showing up out of the blue wasn't some clever plot to see *her*. It was a fluke. A needle-in-a-haystack chance of Yuletide torture. *Just terrific.* She'd spent two entire years patching the shredded remains of her heart to-gether, and just when she'd come to terms with her play-it-safe, hiding-out-in-Idaho lifestyle, Josh had parachuted in and undone years of exacting damage control.

Adrenaline began to surge through her. She tugged at the high ribbing on the neck of her sweater, suddenly wishing she had scrubs on. Why hadn't one of her patients thrown up on her? Then she could have missed this nauseating scene of mistletoe magic. She checked herself. Wishing pa-tients ill wasn't her style, and thankfully the two gastro cases had turned out to be overindulgence rather than food poisoning.

Who ate massive portions of something called Chocolate Decadence and *didn't* expect a sore stomach? People who weren't careful. People who were reckless. People who made decisions on a whim—like Josh.

She made a beeline for the doctors' locker room and grabbed her winter coat before push-ing through the heavy door into the stairwell and pounding up step after step toward the roof, letting out an involuntary wail of relief when she found it was empty.

Silent screams into blankets while trying to re-

tain her control were one thing—but seeing Josh
with another woman... Words couldn't even describe how much it had hurt. Throat-scraping wail
after howl poured out of her throat as the snow bit
at her cheeks and the wind swirled through her hair
and into her tear-blinded eyes. Why had Josh—
of all the people in the world—had to show up?
Hadn't he done enough harm? It was worse than
shock. It was Shock and Awful.

Chest heaving from the effort of purging her
sorrow, Katie forced herself to take more level,
steadier breaths. Knowing a chill could turn into
pneumonia in the blink of an eye at this time of
year, she excavated a woolly hat from the depths
of her pocket. She hadn't let those Girl Scout ses-
sions go to waste.

Prepared at all times. Self-contained at all times.
She tugged on her hat and scowled. Which one
had she left out?

"And a smile in the face of adversity."

Katie's frown deepened. She turned this way
and that, taking in the roof as though she were a
child stuffed into an over-thick snow outfit. The
urge to throw a tantrum was welling within her
again. Twice in one day? Must be a record! Maybe
she should have gone the bad-girl route as a kid. It

might have garnered her a bit more attention from her parents.

She harrumphed. Unlikely.

She pulled out her phone and trawled a finger along the not-very-long list of names to see if there was anyone on there she could talk to. Colleague. Colleague. Colleague. Mentor. Nanny.

Alice Worthing! Her shoulders softened. She had absolutely *loved* her Irish nanny. Alice was the only person she'd told in advance of her elopement, and the second she'd seen the twinkle in the dear woman's eyes, she'd known she was doing the right thing.

Wow—had they both been wrong!

She pushed at the phone symbol anyhow. It would be nice to hear a friendly voice on Christmas Eve.

After a couple of rings she heard laughter and then the lilted *hello* she knew so well. Fifteen years in the US, married to an American for ten of them, and her accent hadn't changed a jot.

"Hello? Is anyone there?"

Katie started. "Sorry, Alice. It's me, Katie Wes— Katie McGann."

"Katie! My sweet Katie. Darlin', how the devil are you? It's been so long. *Too* long! What is it?

Over a year now since you went out west. Are you all right, love? Is everything okay?"

"Yes. Fine." She kicked her boot into the thick rooftop snow.

"Well, that's a lie and we both know it."

Katie smiled at the phone, double-checking that she hadn't video-dialed her friend by accident.

"It's just—I—um—wanted to wish you a merry Christmas."

"Well, that's a lovely sentiment, Katie, but why not tell me the real reason you called?"

"I'd forgotten how quickly you see through me." Katie grinned, now wishing she *had* video-called Alice.

"Well, you and I both know how precious life is, so come on—spit it out."

"Josh."

"Oh, Katie, no—nothing's happened to Josh, has it?"

"No! God, no!" Katie felt surprised at how glad she was that was true. She might not want to be married to him, but she couldn't bear the thought if... "He's shown up at the hospital as my locum."

Another round of laughter followed as Alice called out to her husband, saying Josh had found

Katie. She heard the click of the receiver as Alice's husband got on the line.

"So he finally tracked you down, did he?" James's deep voice rumbled down the line. "He tried to plumb us for info but we didn't breathe a word. We knew you wouldn't want us getting involved. Want me to come out and beat him up for you?"

Katie knew he was joking, but James had always been very protective of her. Her relationship with her own father had never been a close one, so she liked James's concern.

"What sort of nonsense are you talking, man?" Alice hushed him. "Josh's dead romantic. Always was. A bit wild, but showing up on Christmas Eve and all…"

"It wasn't exactly as if they left things on a good note," James riposted.

"Yeah…well…" Katie's mind whirred, trying to catch up with everything as Alice and James bantered. "He came and asked you where I was?"

"Course he did. The boy's mad for you. Always was."

Then why was he trying to kiss Jorja?

Katie and Alice talked for what felt like hours. They had a lot to catch up on. But as the roar of doorbells and barking dogs started to drown out their voices, Katie knew she had to let Alice get back to her own life. She tipped her head to see if she could differentiate between clouds and the falling snow.

"Sorry, Katie. Our little girls' choir has just shown up to sing carols. Please forgive me but I need to go. You'll sort it out for the best. You always do. Lots of love."

"Oh! How is Catherine?"

"She's grand, darlin'. Must dash, but call again soon!"

And the line went dead.

Katie didn't know if she felt better or worse for having made the call. A thousand questions and no answers added to her frustration. She kicked a satisfying lump of snow up into the glowering sky and watched it float back down to the rooftop.

The helicopter hadn't been used in a while, and from the looks of things, the crew hadn't been up yet with the blower. The snow was a good foot deep where she was standing. The drifts were deeper over by the edges. A good three feet by now. Maybe deeper. Winter had started early in Copper Canyon, and no matter how hard they tried to stay on top of the accumulating snow, they couldn't. Which, in this case, was all right. Because it was…beautiful.

She felt the fight go out of her. Maybe that had been her problem all along. Trying too hard to control things. Josh. Herself. She'd even broken down the seven stages of grief, giving herself a month to go through each stage, fastidiously identifying and eradicating anything that would hold back her progress to—to what, exactly?

Josh's angry words came back to her in echoing anvils of self-recognition. *Micromanager. Risk-averse. Exacting perfectionist! Control freak.*

The last one wilted her shoulders into a hunch against the buffeting wind. She looked around the roofscape again, as if it would conjure Josh up from the lower reaches of the hospital so he could call her out himself. Except the only voice she heard those words in was her own. *She* was the one who had shaken off the rest of the words he'd said and turned those remaining into insults. The words she wouldn't let herself remember?

Gorgeous. My love. Sweetheart. Angel. Darlin'.

She blinked away the sting of tears. When things had been good between them, they had been, oh, *so* good. Josh had given her reserves of strength she hadn't known she had. Lit her up like a…oh, the irony…lit her up like a Christmas tree!

She blinked again, feeling a tear drop this time. She swiped it away and tried to shake off the memories. She was in a new place now, and up until the start of this double shift on Christmas Eve, things had been pretty good. Well… She tugged a foot through the snow and stomped toward the roof edge.

Neutral.

How pathetic was that? Even *she* had to snicker at herself. To aspire to have a *neutral* day? Wow! That elite education she'd aced had *really* prepared her for life. She scrunched her eyes tight and forced herself to open them with the promise of seeing something that made her smile.

Not too far away the twinkling lights of Copper Canyon's main street were glittering away like a perfectly decorated window display. The town council always did well. Never too opulent, never mistaking the decor for any holiday other than Christmas. At the far end of Main Street, where the two-lane road split and circled round the town's green, an enormous evergreen twinkled and shone like a bejeweled Fabergé egg through the fat snowflakes swirling around it. At the base of the tree,

Katie could make out the lit outline of the band-stand, its columns rising in twisted swirls of red and white lights.

She reached the edge of the roof and eyed the drift. Higher than she'd thought. Enough snow to cloak the thick safety barriers she knew ran around the edges. She should make a note to hospital admin that they really must be raised—

She checked herself. As far as she knew, she was the only one who was mad enough to come up to the roof in the middle of a snowstorm.

See, universe? Katie McGann can be just as much of a nut burger as the rest of them!

She gave the elements a satisfied grin as she pulled her emergency pair of waterproof mittens from the inner pocket of her down jacket.

Well…pragmatism *was* useful. And it was hardly a storm. A bit of wind. Thick latticed snowflakes big enough to catch on her tongue. She eyed the split-level roof just below her. The empty administrative offices…

She pushed her lips in and out as she considered. Without snow…? Maybe a six-foot drop. With snow…? Hmm…two feet of emptiness before she hit several feet of fluffy virgin snow. Her mind shot back to the rare trips up to her late grandparents' cabin in Vermont, where she, Alice and her grandmother had made endless snow angels.

"Always room for more angels to look out for us." That was how her grandmother had put it. So when she was upset and there was some snow to hand…snow angel. Magic recipe for a better mood.

Would it be fluffy enough to…? *Yeah…why not?* She could throw caution to the wind as easily as the next person…right?

She opened her arms wide, eyed the tilt of the snowdrift, turned around and began to press her weight into her heels. She wobbled for a moment… regained her footing…then reasoned with herself that this was precisely the sort of litmus test she needed to pass in order to prove she could well and truly survive without Josh…beyond *neutral*.

She sucked in a breath and smiled—at the world for just being there and being all snowy and twinkly so that she could make a snow angel when she sure as hell needed one.

As she shifted her heels along the edge again and raised her arms, the door to the stairwell burst open. Josh was calling out her name at ten decibels. His face was a mix of horror and fear when his eyes lit upon her. He called her name again, the vowels bending and elongating in the wind.

"Kaaa-tieee!"

Their eyes connected in a way they never had before. For the first time she saw he had been through it, too. The harrowing, mind-numbing pain of loss. And in that moment she wished back the two years they had spent apart.

Josh watched in horror as Katie's arms windmilled for balance. His eyes raced down her legs as she shifted her heels to regain traction on the icy ledge. Each micro-move she made became overexaggerated with her fruitless efforts to stay upright. Their eyes stayed locked as she completely lost her footing and fell helplessly back into the void.

Never in his life had he felt such searing pain. He had thought the grief at losing his daughter was the worst thing he could have lived through, but losing Katie as well would kill him.

An infinity of darkness spread out before him as he shouted and stumbled toward the edge, not even sure he was making a single sound above the howling in his skull.

Katie's comprehension of the world shifted as her body lost its fight with gravity. Apart from the terror she'd seen in her husband's eyes, she suddenly understood what he meant about the freedom in letting go. Just the release of falling backward was exhilarating.

She opened her throat and screamed as sensations hit her in surreal hits of slow-motion recognition. The breeze swept past her cheeks. She blinked away a snowflake. With the surprise of the fall she'd lost her sense of where she was actually falling. It might have gone on forever.

The sky was astonishingly textured with clouds and the odd hit of stars… When was the last time she'd just looked up and enjoyed the sky?

Before she could take it all in, she hit the powdery snow with a fluffy *ploof!* and lay utterly still as her breath came back to her.

A dim awareness of sound came to her. A male voice. *Josh!* It had to be Josh. Her mind whirled into catch-up mode, her eyes widening as she realized what she was hearing.

"Katie! No!"

Ragged. Rough. Grief-stricken. Why was Josh so upset? She was just making a snow angel, for heaven's sake.

His face appeared over the edge, his features etched with anxiety.

"I fell."

"Yes!" The air came out of his mouth in thick, billowed huffs of breath. "Yes, you did."

"It's nice down here." She saw the sheen of tears rise in his eyes before he had a chance to disguise it as something else. Josh had never been a weeper. He swiped at his eyes with his sleeve. Maybe she'd been mistaken.

"Are you all right?"

Katie could tell Josh was trying to keep his voice under control. Behave as if he saw his estranged wife fall off the edge of a building every day. It suddenly struck her that his reaction was utterly different from what she would have expected. The old Josh would have just leaped over the edge and joined her. Pulled her into his arms and then, after a deep, life-affirming kiss, would have made snow angels with her. Right?

"Katie?" Josh knelt on the ledge and began to scan her acutely for injury. "Are you okay?"

"Pretty good." She moved her arms and legs just a little bit, suppressing a surprise hit of the giggles as she did so. Nothing hurt. She'd landed on an enormous pillow of snow, for heaven's sake! "Actually…" She met his eyes properly this time. "It was pretty fun."

"Fun, huh? Is that what you think? Near enough giving me a heart at—?"

He stopped himself and she watched silently as Josh rearranged his features into a long, studied look before visibly deciding to swallow whatever lecture he'd been about to give. She knew the expression well…and it gave her a hit of understanding she hadn't known she needed. It was the look Josh must have seen on *her* face time and again after they'd lost their baby girl and he'd come back from yet another high-octane experience.

Josh looked away from Katie and gave the vista a scan. The early-evening gloaming left hints of light on the tips of the mountains…gave the glittering Main Street more of a festive punch. His lips thinned as he slowly inhaled and exhaled, trying to get his racing heart under control.

His relief at finding Katie alive and well was morphing into anger. How *dare* she do this? Take such a huge risk? Didn't she know how precious she was to him? His anger welled up further into his chest, searing him from the inside out. *How dare she?*

"A thank-you for stopping you killing yourself might be nice."

"Killing myself?" She pushed herself up to sit and squinted at him through the falling snow. "You think if I—Katie West—Katie McGann," she corrected herself, annoyed, "was going to do something so stupid as to kill myself I'd do it by jumping two feet into a snowdrift?"

"That was difficult to see from the doorway." Josh cleared his throat again and swore under his breath. "So you weren't—?"

"Of course I wasn't. I was just…" She let herself plop back into the lightly compacted drift. "I was just trying to make a snow angel."

She spoke softly. More truculent than apologetic, but, hell, he'd take it. She was alive. That was good enough for now.

He tipped his head to the side and eyed her. "You only make snow angels when you're upset."

"No, I don't!" she shot back, her eyes anywhere but meeting his.

Yup! She was upset. He knew his arrival had upset her, but he hadn't thought launching herself into a snowdrift four floors off the ground would be her response. Maybe he should have called. Scheduled lunch. Done something normal, like she'd been begging him to do all along.

He knelt on the ledge and hitched up his bad leg

before slipping over into the snow mattress Katie was pillowed in. He winced. The old-timers were right about feeling the cold differently once your body had proved itself fallible.

He gave her a grumpy glare and flopped down onto the snow beside her, where they lay in silence for a few moments. He'd thought he'd lost her just now. Lost the love of his life.

Okay, firebrand...cool your jets. You've both had a shock.

He shot a sidelong glance at Katie and saw her all wide-eyed and... *Seriously?* Was she *grinning*? That grin near enough sucker punched the rest of the breath out of his chest and he only just managed to reel in the angry words.

His emotions were running so wild it was impossible to tell if he should just whip out those stupid divorce papers and give her his signature right now. Then maybe they could both get on with their lives.

He swiped at the snowflakes clustering on his lashes. There was no way he could move on. Not like this. Not yet. And if Katie didn't give a monkey's about him she wouldn't be flinging herself off the sides of buildings on Christmas Eve. So...

it was a silver-linings moment. A weird one. But a moment to count himself lucky. Blessed.

It didn't stop him from needing to expunge a bit of "grumpy," though.

Eyes rigidly glued to the heavens, he leveled his voice before starting. "Well, isn't *this* cozy?"

"That's one way of putting it," Katie grumbled.

"This a new Idaho thing? Hurling yourself off the side of buildings without an audience?"

"Something like that."

"Any reason in particular, or did whimsy just overtake you?"

"Yeah," she bit back drily. "That's how I roll. Got it in one, Josh. Crazy Katie West, hitting the fast lane again!"

"West?" He tried not to sound hopeful.

"Whoever."

He let the words settle for a moment. It took one to know one, and she was calling him out. She always read life's instruction book. He barely looked at the book's cover before flinging it away and just going for it. Especially once he'd met his wife. With Katie by his side he had felt invincible.

"It was pretty reckless." He couldn't stop the words choking him as they came out. He sounded like his dad.

"Yeah? Well, the fact you couldn't see the four-foot-deep drift of snow I was aiming for probably gave you the wrong idea. I calculated the risk in advance and determined there was little to no damage that could come to a girl trying her best to have a little *alone time* and make herself a blinking snow angel! And if you want to talk about reckless, you'd better be careful with Jorja. She's got a reputation."

Josh pushed himself up on his elbows and gave her his best *what are you talking about?* look. "Jorja?"

"Yes. Jorja." Her voice went singsong as her hands started to make the beginnings of angel wings in the snow. "Josh and Jorja, sitting in a tree…"

"What are you talking about?"

"The mistletoe?" Her arm movements widened and her legs joined in, occasionally giving his own hand or leg a bash as she worked out her frustration on her snow angel.

"You think I made out with Jorja under some mistletoe?" His voice rang with pure incredulity.

"I *saw* you!" Katie all but snarled.

"No, you did *not*!" Josh retorted, dredging up his best five-year-old's retorts. "You might've seen me standing there—but dodging mistletoe in that hospital of yours is as easy as avoiding patients!"

"Which—by the looks of things—you're doing a pretty good job of. You were hired to work— not to gallop round like an errant King Arthur, swooping up damsels in distress at every hint of a berry! You're a doctor, if my memory serves me correctly! Shouldn't you be behaving responsibly for once? *Doctoring?*"

Katie's words hit him with rapid-fire precision— her body was moving as quickly as she could speak. Josh had never seen her like this—in full flow. Her arms and legs swinging hither and yon. It was going to be one hell of a snow angel.

He couldn't let her words go. Wouldn't stay silent. He was hurting, too. Always had. Putting on a brave face had been the hardest thing he'd done, but he'd thought that was what she'd needed from him.

"You're the one in charge, Katie. Shouldn't you be down there, bossing people around? Making sure everything's in order? Everything in its right place?"

Again and again he'd bitten back words like these in the depths of their grief. But this was Last Chance Saloon time. Despite the widening shock in her dark eyes, the words continued to fly, un-checked, past his lips.

"C'mon, Katie—you always seemed to know what was best for me. What would you advise? What would you suggest I do now?"

"What—what do you mean?" She pushed herself up to stand, distractedly brushing the snow off her clothes, discomfort taking the place of fury.

"You're really good at laying down guidelines. Heaven knows how they're getting on down there without little Miss Perfect dotting the 'I's and crossing the 'T's. How would you *recommend* I comfort myself after seeing my wife take a swan dive off of a building?"

He was all but shouting, rising to his full height before they both awkwardly swung themselves over onto the roof, then stood for who knew how long like two cowboys frozen in a standoff.

"I wasn't—" Katie finally broke the silence then stopped herself, unable to resist glaring at him while she tried to regain her composure. Her common sense.

They'd had a variation on this fight a thousand times and she didn't have it in her to have it again. Didn't want to. She'd seen the fear in his eyes and she'd never meant to be cruel to him. Not then.

Not now. But this very moment was proof positive that they couldn't be together. Not when they couldn't even bring a bit of good out of the other as they had once done. They needed to wrap this up. It was the only way to go forward.

"Why are you here, Josh? What exactly is it that you want?"

"You," he answered. "I came here because I want *you*."

The air between them grew electric. With unspoken words. Unspent desire.

His blue eyes told her a thousand things at once. Gone was the recrimination. The anger. In their place was the heady, crackling energy that had never failed to draw them together. Katie hadn't realized how much she missed Josh on a physical level.

He didn't wait for an invitation.

Two of his long-striding steps and he'd pulled her up and into his arms. All thought was gone. She was reduced to sensation only, such was the power of his touch. She felt his lips against hers, both urgent and tender. Her every pore ached with the immediacy of her body's response to his touch. Winter jackets, woolen hats, leather gloves—none of the clunky gear of the season detracted from the pure, undiluted hunger Katie was experiencing.

Somewhere out there in the far reaches of her mind she knew she should be pushing him away. Knew she shouldn't be returning hungry kiss after kiss, each one filled with two years' worth of need. His hands cupped her jaw as the kisses grew deeper still. A low moan met one of his as they pressed tightly against the other. Everything felt familiar and new—as it always had—but their connection was… It felt unbreakable. Timeless.

Had she been wrong to send him away?

A vibration jostled at her waistline. Her pager.

Another one sounded. Josh's.

She pulled back, wondering if her mouth looked as bruised with kisses as Josh's did. Her fingers fumbled with the pager, her eyes still glued to her husband's face.

He was part of her. She knew that now. Making him leave had been ridiculous. No amount of time or distance could sever the ties between them. But what they had wasn't healthy. Wasn't meant for long-term—especially if she were ever, one day, to hold a baby of her own in her arms.

"Multiple injuries. We'd better get down there."

"What?" Katie shook her head clear of the "Josh and baby" fog.

"Read your pager. Ambulances are due in a few minutes."

"Right. Yes." She grabbed her phone from her pocket, relieved it hadn't been lost to the snow-drift in her snow-angel frenzy, and punched out the numbers of the ER desk. "It's Dr. McGann. Are the teams setting up the trauma units?"

Josh watched as Katie listened, responded, thumbed away the stray wisps of lipstick from around her mouth and tugged her clothes back into place. Moment by moment she became Dr. McGann again. This reinvention of herself who was all business. The Katie he'd first met. Not the one who came alive each time they touched or when their eyes lit upon the other. *This* Katie's eyes were near enough devoid of life. His heart ached to put back each and every spark he knew lay dormant within them. Now wasn't the time.

He shifted his hips. His body was trying to fight down the force of desire kissing Katie had elicited in him. She felt good. Ridiculously good in his arms. It made the idea of Paris even more insane if she weren't by his side.

The peal of ambulance sirens became faintly audible.

If he'd had a spare half hour he would have made a snowman up here and then kung fu'd its head off. It would have been satisfying. For about a second.

He shook his head and took up the pace Katie was setting to the roof door. At least he knew work would keep him distracted for the next hour or five, depending upon how bad the traumas were. Snow and automobiles? The onset of darkness on Christmas Eve, when everyone's expectations were just a little bit higher than any other time of year…? Yeah. It wasn't going to be pretty. Not in the slightest.

CHAPTER FOUR

KATIE STOPPED IN her tracks. Now, *this* she certainly hadn't expected. The first ambulance had pulled into the covered bay with a horse trailer attached to it, and the crew, along with the help of a teary girl dressed up as the Virgin Mary, were unloading a donkey.

"Can you help Eustace, please?" the girl wailed when her eyes lit on Katie.

Eustace the donkey?

"Ooh! A nativity donkey!" Jorja appeared alongside Katie, rubbing her hands together and blowing on them as her feet sashayed her from side to side.

"I think we'd better take a look at *you* first." Katie's eyes were on the girl who, through the folds of her costume, was clutching her side. "What's your name, hon?"

"Maddie."

"What a lovely name! Is there anyone you can leave in charge of the—Eustace—while we bring you inside?"

"No!" The girl's eyes widened in fear, and as she and the donkey stepped into the bright light of the ambulance bay outside the ER, Katie could see she also had a cut on her forehead over what appeared to be a growing lump. "I am not leaving Eustace. He is my best friend and we have to get to Bethlehem tonight!"

"Maybe we can find a hitching post for Eustace."

"But he's bleeding!"

"What have we got here?"

Josh's voice shot along Katie's nervous system as she approached Maddie. Her fingers flew automatically to her lips, and she wished the remembered pulse of their kisses weren't so vivid. She pushed down the thoughts and forced herself to focus. A Mary intent on getting to Bethlehem and a donkey with quite a serious cut to his haunch. Hospital protocol to adhere to...

A lightbulb went off. Josh's passion for medicine had come about by fixing the local wildlife and working under the wing of the country vet on the ranch his father had managed. It wasn't really playing by the rulebook, but... Were there different rules at Christmas? Or at least a bit of Yuletide flexibility? The emergency vets were on the other side of town, and using ambulances to tow livestock trailers had already been done—

"What do you say we pop you on a gurney, Maddie? Out here? That way Dr. McGann can take a look at you and I can stitch up… What did you say your pal's name was?"

Mind reader.

"Eustace!" Maddie replied with a broad smile, then another wince.

"Eustace! I had an Uncle Eustace, and he was as stubborn as a mule. Did you say your Eustace was a mule or a donkey?"

"A donkey! Can't you tell the difference?" Maddie giggled through her pain.

Katie couldn't fight the smile his words brought. Josh's way with patients—especially children— had always been second to none. He still had the magic touch. Something she'd worked hard at and never fully achieved. Especially after the baby.

The thought instantly sobered her. They had two or even three more ambulances due in from the same crash, so they needed to get down to business, bedside manner or no. Maddie's parents, or whoever had been driving the truck pulling the trailer, must be incoming. Otherwise they surely would have shown up with Maddie and Eustace.

"Jorja, can you—?"

"Already on it!" the nurse called, halfway through the electric doors.

"Hey, fellas!" Josh was signaling to the ambulance drivers to move the livestock trailer outside of the bay so the other ambulances would have room to pull in when they arrived.

Katie's two interns had appeared, with a gurney each, and Jorja had shouldered an emergency medical kit.

"Where would you like this one, Dr. McGann?" asked Michael. She smiled gratefully at the curly-haired intern and pointed over to a well-lit spot by the sliding doors. He was quiet—very committed and ultraserious. Birds of a feather. They got on well.

"Make sure those brakes are on." She pointed at the gurney wheels. If they needed to whisk Maddie inside for any reason, they could—but out here they needed to be as safe as possible.

"Where are your parents, honey?"

"Be careful with his halter." Maddie's eyes were glued on Josh as he expertly knotted Eustace to a pillar, petting and soothing the donkey, who seemed also to have fallen under Josh's spell. *Dr. Doolittle strikes again!*

Maddie threw tips at Josh for keeping Eustace happy, her fears about his welfare quelled by his verbal updates. Katie gave an internal sigh of relief. If Maddie had been in that livestock trailer when the crash happened, she was bound to have had a heck of a knock, and inspections for broken ribs were less than fun. If she was properly distracted that would help.

"We're going to put a little numbing agent on Eustace's rump, here. Is that all right, Maddie? Do we need your parents' permission to go ahead and give him stitches?"

Katie shot him a look. She received a nod of response. One that said he knew what was going on and was playing the Distraction Whilst Gathering Information Game.

"Michael," she whispered, "can you get me some scissors, please? We need to cut these off." Katie needed to get the layers of robes off Maddie without moving her ribs. If she lifted the robes off over the girl's head and there had been any acute breaks or internal injuries, the movement might make things worse. Broken ribs were one thing… Punctured lungs were a whole new kettle of fish.

"Dr. McGann." Shannon, her other intern, tapped her on the shoulder, magically appearing with a pair of scissors in hand. "A second ambulance is five minutes out. They've got a male patient presenting with suspected fractured wrist and extensive leg injuries and another young adult male presenting with a broken nose and other minor injuries from an air bag."

Katie nodded whilst deftly dividing the robes of Maddie's costume. The girl's face was growing paler, and the sooner she could get her lying down for an examination the better. "Want to give me a hand here, Shannon?"

"Sure, but don't you want me to do the incoming—?"

Shannon was always keen to be first on scene for whatever "A-list" injuries came through the emergency room doors, but Katie had been very careful to divvy them out between her gore-hungry intern and Michael, whose "ladies first" attitude Katie hadn't quite figured out. Nervous or just genuinely polite?

Tonight wasn't about politics, though. It was about priority.

"If you could help me get Maddie out of these robes and then make sure there are two triage areas prepped, nurses on standby with gurneys and a couple of wheelchairs, that would be great. There doesn't sound like much the EMTs won't be able to handle in terms of stabilizing. Let X-Ray know someone will be on the way up."

Shannon's lips pursed in disappointment, and Katie knew better than to think the evening would run smoothly. If you relaxed, things went south. That was how it worked in an ER. That was how it worked in life.

"Ouch!" Maddie gasped and wobbled.

Katie and Shannon each reached for an elbow as the last of the biblical robes dropped away. Maddie's hands flew to her side, where blood was seeping through her shirt, and Eustace brayed softly, as if he knew his owner was in pain.

"You cut my robes?" Maddie was properly tearful now.

"Easy there, boy. I just need you to stay steady," Josh was saying.

"It's all right, honey. We can get those stitched back up for you—no problem."

Katie's eyes flicked back to Josh as he made a general callout for an electric shaver. The donkey's winter coat was making the topical numbing agent less effective, and she could tell he was trying to play by the rules as much as possible. They could use xylocaine without too many questions.

But proper injectable painkillers...? Less easy to explain where vials of lidocaine were—much less to write up a chart for Eustace. Off the books was best—even if it bent the rules.

Katie thought for a second of stopping him. This was how doctors got fired. Risks. She never took risks. Josh never needed to think twice about it.

"Nurse!" he called, without looking up from what he was doing.

Katie flinched infinitesimally as Jorja appeared by Josh's side in an instant. He had said it was all a mistake. The mistletoe mishap...

She pulled her gaze back to Maddie, whose eyes were widening at the sight of the blood on her white shirt.

"It's all right, Maddie. Let's get you up on the gurney, honey." She looked at Michael, who had arrived back at Maddie's other side. "On three." They eased Maddie up and onto the gurney on her count. "Right! Let's check you out. I'm going to have to lift up your shirt, and it's pretty cold out here. Are you sure you don't want to go inside?"

"No!" There was no mistaking the determination in the girl's voice. "Where Eustace goes, I go." She twisted suddenly, trying to get a better look at her pricked-eared pal. Her eyes tightened with pain. "It hurts to breathe."

Fear suddenly entered the little girl's eyes. She couldn't be more than eleven…but Katie was sure an old soul was fueling her.

"Lie down again, hon. I think you might've bruised a couple of ribs. Michael, could you get me a couple of blank—?"

"Already on it, Doc."

Katie rucked up Maddie's shirt, relieved to see the bleeding was from a gash and nothing more. But in a dirty livestock trailer? They'd have to put a booster tetanus shot on the girl's tick-list as well.

She tried to go for Josh-casual. "Say, it looks like you and Eustace are both going to be getting stitches tonight."

A grin lit up the girl's face. "Really?"

Hmm… Josh-casual obviously works.

A sting of guilt shot through her at the words she had flung at him when things had seemed too dark to continue. *Reckless. Unthinking. Careless.* Maybe his laissez-faire attitude had been to soothe her. To comfort her in a time of great sorrow.

She swallowed hard and continued her examination of Maddie.

"That hurts!" Maddie yelped.

"That's your rib cage acting up. Where exactly were you when the accident happened?"

"With Eustace."

Katie's eyes widened, her suspicions confirmed. *Well, that was just about as health and safety unconscious as things got.*

"And your parents let you ride in there?"

Maddie's eyes began to dart around the covered area. "Not exactly..."

"Who was driving the tow vehicle?"

"My bro—" She reconsidered giving the information, swallowing the rest of the word. Tears sprang into her eyes. "Am I going to get in trouble?"

"No, honey. Of course not. But riding in trailers with live—with Eustace—isn't really legal."

"Are my brothers going to jail?"

Katie's eyes shot across to meet Josh's, but he was one hundred percent focused as stitch after stitch brought the sides of the cut on Eustace's rump neatly together. She had always loved watching Josh's hands at work. They were large, capable hands. The intricate work they completed with skillful dexterity always surprised her.

Just as easy to picture him whipping a lasso into action as he had when he was a boy as it was to see him deftly tying a miniature knot at the end of a row of immaculate stitches as he was now.

"Probably best if you keep pneumonia out of the symptoms…"

Josh didn't look up as he spoke, but he had always had a second sense for when Katie's eyes were trained on him. She stiffened. It wasn't often he had to remind her to keep her eye on the ball. The role reversal didn't sit well.

"Maddie?" Josh raised his voice a bit. "Eustace is doing pretty good, here. Mind if I snaffle him some carrots from somewhere, then let him have a bit of a lie-down in the trailer?"

"That would be nice." Maddie sniffled, her fear and pain visibly kicking up a notch. "There are carrots already in the trailer."

"Michael." Katie snapped into action. "Let's tuck these blankets round Maddie and get her a tetanus shot before bringing her up to X-Ray, please, to check on her ribs. Maddie, honey, Michael's going to need your parents' phone number so we can get in touch—just to okay any treatment you're going to need, all right?"

"You're not going to let them arrest my brothers, are you? We just wanted to get to the nativity early!"

Tears began to pour out of Maddie's blue eyes and Katie's heart all but leaped to her throat. There was such love and protectiveness in her words. "Why don't we take things one at a time? We'll call your parents, sort you out, and then deal with everything else as and when it happens."

"Do you think there will be an angel looking after my brothers?"

"Dr. McGann?" Jorja stuck her head through the sliding doors. "That second ambulance is incoming."

"I sure do, Maddie," said Katie. And she meant it. "This is Michael—Dr. Rainer. He's going to take you up to X-Ray. We'll see you in a little bit, all right?"

"Okay…" The young girl snuffled. Her head turned to find Josh within sight. "Thanks for looking after Eustace."

"You bet, kiddo. It was my pleasure." Josh flashed her one of his warm smiles and gave her arm a quick squeeze before Michael and a nurse wheeled her off to the ER.

The wail of the sirens grew louder and Katie ripped off her protective gloves, quickly wiggling her fingers into the fresh pair one of the nurses handed her. If she'd thought things had been busy earlier, they were going into full-time Christmas Eve Crazy now the sun had set.

"Teenage male, presenting with multiple leg injuries and compound fracture to the wrist."

"Got it." Josh helped unload the gurney along with the EMT. This was Chris, Maddie's older brother.

Josh took in the EMT's rattle of information as he scanned the teen's face again. Chris couldn't have had his first whiskers for long, let alone gained much experience behind the wheel in a snowstorm.

A nurse met him at the doors and took over as the EMT finished reeling off the treatments Chris had already received. His injuries were severe. Compound fracture to the femur. Possible compression to the ankle. Severe dislocation of the knee. And who knew what muscles and ligaments might have been torn or burst? He'd be off that leg for months. Minimum. From the looks of the blood loss and extensive damage, the boy would need to be in surgery sooner rather than later. No time to wait for parental consent.

"Right, we'd better take a look at the mess you've made of yourself."

"Where's Maddie?" The boy's eyes were wide with panic.

"It's all right, buddy. Maddie is up in X-Ray. Looks like you messed your leg up pretty well."

"Where's my brother? Have you seen Nick? Where's Maddie? Is Eustace all right?"

A gurney went past with one of the interns at the helm. The keen one. Shannon…? Didn't matter.

"Hey, bro!"

Another teenage boy called from a gurney as he was wheeled past. Blood was smeared all over his face and winter coat. This was obviously the one with the broken nose.

"You haven't given them Mom and Dad's number, have you?" he shouted, before his gurney turned the corner to one of the triage areas.

"No way—what do you think I am? An idio—? *Ow!*" The scream Chris emitted filled the corridor, and just as quickly as the howl of acute pain had taken over the soundscape, it disappeared as Chris lapsed into unconsciousness.

"Anyone think to check on the femoral artery?"

Josh didn't know why he was asking. There was blood everywhere, the EMTs were long gone, and the nurse had been with him for no more than a few seconds.

"Let's skip triage and get straight up to surgery—"

"Only for a handover." Katie's voice broke in.

"This guy's going to bleed out if we don't get him on a table fast. And who knows what sort of filth is in that leg? Time's against us, Katie."

"Yes, it is. And that's why we're going to let one of the orthopedic surgeons cover this one. They're already prepping the room."

Josh nodded curtly. He thrived on make-or-break surgery, and if there was one person in the world who knew that was true of him, she was standing right there looking the picture of officiousness.

"We need you in Trauma, Josh. There are more patients incoming. The rescue crews only just opened up the car that got hit by the snowplow."

"Understood."

And he did. Katie did prioritizing. He did gut instinct. It was why they had always worked together so well. The yin to the other's yang. Sure, there were fiery moments—but balance always won out in the end.

Well… He watched as she flew past him into one of the cubicles, where a patient could be heard arguing with one of the nurses. He scrubbed his jaw hard. Balance hadn't *always* won out in the end.

He gave the nurse on the other side of the gurney a tight smile.

"Let's get this whippersnapper up to surgery so we can get back for the incomings."

"You bet, Dr. West."

"Mrs. Wilson goes into Three and Mr. Wilson into Four." Katie was issuing directions faster than a New York traffic cop in rush hour. She was in a fury. The Wilsons had been the hardest hit but had been the last to be brought in.

"It took the fire crew a while to dislodge their car from the snowplow."

"One more patient incoming!"

Michael was hurtling down the corridor with a gurney. Gone was his quiet, serene demeanor. He looked near wild with panic. For an instant Katie thought the gurney was empty and that her reliable intern had all but lost the plot entirely—until she saw the tiny figure lying on the gurney. A little girl. She looked about three.

The same age her daughter would have been if she had lived. The hollow ache of grief began to creep into Katie's heart. Josh appeared on the other side of the gurney. *Great. Just what she needed.*

The one person in the world who could make these feelings multiply into Infinityville.

"What have we got here?"

"Three-year-old girl presenting with abdominal bruising and pain, blood in the urine, internal bleeding—suspected trauma to the left kidney."

Michael rattled out a few more details as they raced the gurney toward the trauma unit.

"Can we get her into OR Two with Dr. Hastings?" Katie kept her eyes trained on Michael. This was a nightmare blossoming out of control.

"Nope. He's busy with an emergency appendectomy."

This little girl couldn't wait. If her kidney was bleeding out, she needed surgery immediately or she would die. Her eyes flicked from Michael to Josh.

"What about Dr. Hutchins?"

"They're all busy, Dr. McGann." Michael churned out the information, oblivious to the emotional storm brewing between Katie and Josh. "We've prepped OR Four for you. Do you need me to assist?"

Katie's eyes widened. She blinked, doing her utmost to wear her best poker face. All the other surgeons were busy. She'd have to do it—keep this child alive. She felt her hands go clammy as they clutched the side rails of the gurney. Her heart rate quickened and she knew if she looked into a mirror right now she would see her pupils were dilating.

"Are you up to doing a nephrectomy?" Josh's voice was low. Not accusatory—the tone *she* would have used for someone out of their depth. Safety was paramount, particularly with lawsuits swinging like an evil pendulum above their every move these days.

"Of course!" she bit back.

Josh accompanied her, uninvited, into the lift on the way to the surgical ward, dismissing Michael from gurney duty with a smile.

"It's a routine surgery. I did one last week."

But not on a child...a little girl. And not with you here.

Katie didn't dare meet his eyes. If she was going to keep it together to save this little girl's life, a shot of Josh's deep blue eyes was exactly what would have calmed her three years ago. That time had long passed. Even so, she could almost see her heart pumping beneath the scrubs she'd tugged on after Snow-Angel-Gate.

She couldn't help herself. As the doors slid closed and the pair of them were left alone with their tiny patient, she lifted her eyes to meet his. They said everything she had wanted to see in them when they'd lost their little girl.

I'm here for you. You can trust in me. Let me help you.

"Don't worry. I've got this." Katie ripped her eyes away from his. "You should go back down. If anything major happens in the ER—"

"If anything major happens in the ER," he interrupted, "they will page us. I'm staying with you."

"What are you saying, Josh?" Katie couldn't keep the disbelief out of her voice. "Are you saying I'm not up to this?"

"No," he began carefully. "I'm saying you've had a long day, a couple of shocks, and whether you like it or not, you need me by your side. I'll just stay for a minute or so—until you get going."

The elevator doors opened before Katie could reply. Which was just as well. Because what could she say other than *You're right*?

She had struggled over the past three years, doing operations that reminded her of her little girl and the life she might have had. Earlier on she'd deftly handed over any critical surgeries on young children to her colleagues. Just being responsible for the delicate life of a child had been too overwhelming—her own body had proved she didn't have what it took to care for one. But in the past year she'd taught herself to close down—to behave like the clinician she was.

But with Josh here…? Game-changer. She had to prove to him she was over it. Over *him*. That she had moved on from the loss of their child.

Elizabeth.

Elizabeth Rose West.

A beautiful name for their darling little girl, who was nothing more than a statistic now. One out of seventy mothers give birth to a stillborn baby in America every day. The volume of that annual loss was almost too much to bear. She'd never even bothered to check the statistics on failed marriages in the wake of such a loss. Just shut it all out and moved away.

Katie gritted her teeth and gave her head a quick shake. Cobwebs and history didn't belong in there now. This child's life depended upon clear, swift thinking.

The anesthetist met her at the OR door for a quick handover. "A necrotomy?" He tipped his head toward the little girl.

"'Fraid so." Katie tried to keep her tone bright.

"Well, you did a great job with the last one—no reason this should be any different."

"Thanks, Miles. I appreciate it."

"Well, if you'll both excuse me, I'll go in with the patient and get the anesthetics in order."

"Sure thing. Oh! This is Josh. He's—" *Er...my husband, and I still love him, and...*

"Dr. West." Josh jumped in to rescue her. Again. "Locum over the holiday period. I would shake hands, but—" He gestured at the gurney he was trying to navigate into the OR.

"Miles Brand. Good to meet you." He took over moving the gurney, along with a nurse who had materialized from the OR. "Let's get this girl inside and on the table, shall we?"

"I'm going to scrub in while she's prepped," Katie said needlessly after he'd left.

"I'll join you," Josh offered with a soft smile.

An encouraging one. One she should graciously accept. Because what was happening right now was ticking all the I'm-Not-Ready-For-This boxes she'd systematically arranged in her brain's no-go area.

"Thanks."

They pushed into the scrub room together, shoulders shifting against each other's as they had back in the day.

Josh allowed himself a millisecond of pleasure before he realigned his focus. Covert calming. It was his specialty.

"What's the layout here?"

"Near enough the same as Boston," Katie answered, pointing out the shelves that held surgical caps and masks.

Their eyes met as she tugged on a standard blue surgical cap.

"Where's the one I got you?" It had been covered in wildflowers. What she smelled of, he'd told her when she'd unwrapped it.

"In the wash."

Her eyes flicked away and he knew she was lying.

He tried not to notice her tying on her face mask in an effort to hide the painful thickets of emotion she was stumbling through.

Never mind, sweetheart. I feel it, too.

Stepping up to the sink, they both let muscle memory take over. The warm, steady flow of water was the predominant sound in the room as he and Katie took a good five minutes to systematically wash and scrub, first their nails, then their hands, which they held above the level of their elbows to prevent dirty water from dripping onto them.

Josh hit the taps with his elbows when they'd both finished. Katie nodded at the stack of sterile hand towels—one for each arm.

"You sure you're good?" He handed her a towel.

"Medicine is the only thing I *am* sure of these days."

Two nurses pushed into the scrub room with gowns before he could reply. There was room for hope in her response. Room to believe he was right to have sought her out. His lips parted into a smile for which he received a quick, grim nod.

Fine. He felt he'd been thrown a buoy. He could work with a nod.

She could do this, Katie silently assured herself. She'd done it before, and she would do it again.

"Arm," instructed the surgical nurse.

Katie stuck her arm into the sterilized blue sleeve and made a one-eighty twist to fully secure the surgical gown around her, finding herself standing face-to-face with Josh while his gown was tied. He arched an inquisitive eyebrow.

Are you ready? it said.

She arched one back. Hadn't they been through this?

"Left hand, please, Dr. McGann."

She lifted it up and widened her eyes to a glare. Why didn't he stop *smiling*?

"And the right."

Katie raised her hand, holding her arm taut as the nurse tugged on the glove. The other nurse was clearly pleased she had won Josh in the surgeon crapshoot.

"Thank you, Marilyn. Merry Christmas to you."

"Merry Christmas to you, too, Dr. West." The nurse giggled.

Katie frowned. How on earth did he know *Marilyn*?

She had half a mind to step across the small room and lick Josh's gloved hands, rendering him unclean for the surgery.

Childish? Yes. Something the head of the ER should do right before surgery? Probably not.

There was a life to save—and she was going to be the doctor who saved it.

CHAPTER FIVE

"ARE YOU DOING it open or laparoscopically?" Josh kept his voice low and steady. Curious.

"Open."

Katie's eyes flicked to his as he skirted the periphery of the surgical team gathering in the OR.

"Unusual."

Not for his girl, but he knew she was always at her calmest when she talked systematically through her surgery.

Katie nodded. Blinked. His heart skipped a beat before she responded in a clear voice.

"Not in a trauma like this. Laparoscopically is better for routine."

She wasn't saying anything he didn't know, but with a team of people in the room, communicating with a nod or a look wasn't good enough. Everyone had to be on the same page or mistakes would be made.

"There is potentially a lot of other damage in

here, and we're better off with a clear view of what we're dealing with."

"Rib removal?" one of the surgical nurses asked, indicating that she wanted to have the correct instruments to hand.

"Hopefully not, but one could've been broken on impact. We'll have to check."

Katie was grateful other members of the OR team were chiming in. She knew Josh's steady, careful breakdown of the steps in the guise of "reminding himself" was to keep her mind off the tiny body lying on the operating table. Josh could have done this surgery in his sleep. So could she. And he was just reminding her of what was true.

"A partial nephrectomy with so much damage could lead to the need for another surgery," Katie continued. "I don't want that for her. I won't know until I see the damage, but radical is the best option to keep things minimal for—"

"Casey," volunteered one of the nurses as the little girl's body was stabilized for Katie to make the first incision. "Casey Wilson's her name. The parents sent up her information when you were scrubbing in."

Perfect. A name. Just the way to keep it clinical.

Her grip tightened on the scalpel. "I'm preparing to make the incision."

"The bruising certainly indicates massive trauma."

"The EMTs said the snowplow hit her side of the car. She's lucky to have survived at all."

Katie shook away this new piece of information as she made an eight-inch cut from the front of the girl's soft belly to just below her small rib cage. Her mind began to take over, and her heart beat with a steadier cadence. A clock could have marked time with her breaths.

Massive trauma to one kidney. The other, thankfully, was untouched.

She switched instruments and began to cut and move muscle, tiny pieces of fat and the collection of tissue that held the kidney in place. It was steady, systematic work. A glance at the stats here. A minute cut and stitch there. Updates from the nurses. Eyes fastidiously avoiding the tiny little girl's head, just beyond the surgical drape. A vague awareness of Josh moving opposite her at the surgical table.

As she guided her hands through the surgery, it hit her how quickly she'd lapsed into deriving comfort from Josh's rock-solid presence across the table from her. From the moment before she'd stepped into the OR, when fear had threatened to compromise all that she worked so hard for, even the tiniest of tremors she had felt in her hands had left her. And something deep within her heart told her it was having the man she'd once believed to be the love of her life with her.

She flicked her eyes up to meet his. Blue, pure, unwavering. He nodded before returning his eyes to the operation. There was severe bruising along Casey's rib cage—no doubt from the seat belt—but the kidney seemed to have taken the bulk of the trauma. Katie worked her way around the tiny organ, taking particular care to properly clamp and seal the blood vessels before ultimately and successfully removing the kidney.

Textbook.

"You want me to close?" It was an offering, not a doubt about her ability.

Katie shook her head. "I'm good." She'd made it this far. She was going to see it through.

Again, muscle memory took over as she pulled the surgical area back together, minus the small kidney, with a series of immaculately executed stitches. She ran the nurses through the aftercare before allowing herself another glance across the operating table.

"See?"

Josh's blue eyes twinkled at her. Katie could tell from the crinkles round them he was smiling.

"You did it."

"You ready for Secret Santa?" Jorja, despite nearing the end of a sixteen-hour shift, seemed just as sprightly as she had when Josh had first met her.

Was she rechargeable?

"Sure thing."

"We're all meeting down at the central desk at midnight." Jorja's hand shot up to cover her mouth as she stifled a yawn.

Ah! She was human.

Josh kept a good arm's length between them as they walked down the corridor toward the ER. He didn't want any more misunderstandings under the mistletoe. He'd tried dating a couple of times after he'd decided the only way forward was moving on, but had never got past ordering a drink before faking a pager call. Cheap trick, but faking affection would have been worse.

But that didn't mean he couldn't be chatty.

"This was a long shift for you. A double?"

"No longer than yours."

She nodded her head in acknowledgment. "I do it every year." She continued when Josh raised his eyebrows. "So I can be with my family on Christmas Day."

"Oh, right! So you're a local?"

"Yup." She nodded, her voice swelling with pride. "Born and bred Copper Creeker. All six of my brothers and sisters, too."

"Six!" Josh couldn't keep the surprise out of his voice.

"Yup!" Jorja chirped again. "It means the turkey has to be absolutely ginormous—so my brothers have started deep-frying it outside to keep the oven clear for Mom."

"Sounds good."

Jorja brightened. "Want to come? You're welcome. Everyone brings a boyfriend or a girlfriend."

Josh widened the gap between them. "Oh, no. No, thanks. Not for me. I'm on shift. Thanks, though."

Jorja's smile faltered a bit. Josh scrubbed a hand through his hair. She was a nice enough girl, but... But he already had a girl. The girl of his dreams. And he was a little busy proving to her how indispensable he was.

"It was a lovely invitation—it's just…"

"Don't worry." She stopped to pick a piece of errant tinsel off the floor and wove it round and round her finger, turning it pale, then pink again… pale, then pink.

"I'm sorry, Jorja." Josh checked an instinct to reach out and give her shoulder a comforting squeeze.

"I saw how you looked at Dr. McGann when we were under the mistletoe."

This time Josh really *was* surprised. He didn't know he'd been that obvious.

"You two know each other from before, don't you?"

That was one way to put it.

"We met in medical school."

Jorja discarded the tinsel in a bin and gave a wistful sigh. "It's always the good ones who are taken!"

Responding to that might be awkward.

"Hey!" The young woman's features brightened again as she tugged her errant ponytail back into place. "Who'd you get for your Secret Santa?"

"Isn't that supposed to be secret?"

"Yeah—but wouldn't it be fun if you got Dr. McGann?"

Josh considered for a moment and then lifted an eyebrow to indicate that, yes, there just *might* be some fun there...

"Here!" She dug into her nurse's smock and pulled out a crisply folded bit of paper. "I got Dr. McGann. Who'd *you* get?"

"Didn't you get her a present already?" Josh fought the urge to seem too keen.

"Oh, I just snagged a plateful of my grandma's Christmas cookies. She makes an amazing selection. Snickerdoodles, gingerbread men, buckeyes, peppermint crunch—you name it, she makes it."

"She sounds like my Gramma Jam-Jam! Never met a Christmas cookie she didn't like."

Her passing had been like losing a limb. Another loss he'd had to deal with without Katie by his side. It struck him that this mission was about more than trust. He'd known the second Katie had laid eyes on him that she still loved him. What they had was chemical. No amount of spreadsheets or flowcharts or "stages of grief" steps were going to take the connection they had away.

But this little reunion had brought more questions than answers so far. He knew in his heart that she could trust him. But when he'd needed her most she'd upped and left. Could he trust her to stick by him if things got tough again?

"Dr. West?"

Josh could see Jorja was talking to him, but did he have a clue about what? Not one.

Jorja threw her hands up in the air. "Typical man! Concentration factor…nil! No wonder I can't get a boyfriend. I can't even get a male to *listen* to me, let alone like me."

She swatted his arm, bringing his focus back to her. Again. *Oops.*

"Sorry, Jorja—I didn't quite catch what you said."

"Yeah," she deadpanned. "I got *that*. I was asking who your Secret Santa was so we can trade. If you still want to."

"Well…it sounds like—" he dug his scrap of paper out of his lab coat pocket and read "—Dr. Michael Rainer is going to be one lucky guy… having a plate of your grandmother's cookies all to himself."

"Michael…" She said the intern's name as if she were tasting it and wasn't entirely sure what she thought of it. Then clearly a decision was made. "Michael." She said it again, this time looking as though she'd just enjoyed a delicious bite of peppermint candy.

Josh grinned. Michael might have to watch himself around the mistletoe. He threw an arm round the nurse's shoulders and gave her a quick squeeze. This Secret Santa swap could be just what he needed.

Katie nodded at the cleared ER board with a satisfied smile. It probably wouldn't last long—but even a few moments of clean board always lifted her heart.

"Someone looks happy. Did the surgery go well?"

Michael appeared at her side, giving her a little jump.

"Yes." Katie nodded, feeling the weight of the success lighten her heart. "Yes, it really did."

And it meant more than anyone will know.

Well. One person would know.

She heard Josh's laugh before she saw him—and the hit of response in her belly shifted the charge of success into something more electric. It didn't take a doctor to know it was pure unadulterated attraction. It was adrenaline from the surgery, she reasoned. It would pass.

"Right!" Katie went into efficiency mode. "We've got both shift groups together. Quick reminder: Secret Santa gifts go into lockers, please— not here in the reception area."

A nurse guiltily tucked the foil package she'd been edging onto the counter back into her pocket.

Katie gave her lower lip a guilty scrape with her teeth. She hated being a Scrooge, but this *was* a place of work.

"Good work on clearing the board after a pretty hectic run. A couple of patients are in Recovery after surgery, but there's no one unexpected in Intensive, thanks to you all."

A smattering of applause filled the area around the central desk. The staff looked tired, but triumphant. Shannon—her keenest intern—for once looked as if she'd had enough. Michael still looked doggedly studious, but she could see the fatigue in his eyes when he pulled off his glasses and gave them a rub. A few of the nurses were hiding yawns. Most of them, actually.

They'd all been through the wringer and Katie didn't feel any different.

Despite her best intentions, Katie locked her eyes with Josh's. She might not have made it through surgery without him by her side and he knew it. It made her feel vulnerable and protected at the same time. The look in his eyes made her breath catch in her throat. Pure, undiluted love.

Saying goodbye at the end of this shift was going to be harder than she'd thought.

Her eyes widened, still holding the pure blue magic of Josh's gaze. *She hadn't called the agency for a replacement!* And, realistically, was there going to be a locum tenens out there in the mountainscape of Copper Canyon—or anywhere in Idaho—willing to tear themselves away from whatever they'd planned to do with their family over the holidays?

When she and Josh had had the holidays off they'd been inseparable. In more ways than one.

She hunched her shoulders up and down. She was just going to have to suck it up. Getting a replacement for Josh at this juncture was about as likely as Santa Claus walking through the sliding doors.

"Where *is* he?"

A huge gust of wind and winter storm burst into the waiting room, along with a bearded man dressed in full Santa regalia with a rosy-cheeked Mrs. Claus following in his wake.

"Where's my son?" the bearded man roared again.

Temperatures often ran high in the ER, and it looked like Santa's temper was soaring.

"What's your son's name, sir?" Josh was by his side in an instant—with a mix of concerned doctor and *Watch yourself, Santa* in his tone and body language. Josh was tall, and he had the confident carriage of a rodeo cowboy. Santa, however, seemed immune to what had all but buckled her knees.

"Klausen. Check your list, Doc. Check it twice if you have to!"

If Katie hadn't been so taken aback by Mr. Klausen's arrival, she would have tittered at this similarity to a certain red-suited fellow who, by all accounts, should be pretty busy shooting down chimneys about now.

"Chris Klausen," the man bit out.

His tone was so sharp Katie choked on her giggles.

"I've seen the trailer in the parking lot. It's the busiest night of the year and I *know* they've got Eustace in there. The nativity was a shambles!"

"Dad?" Maddie appeared round the corner, a bandage on her head, her arms wrapped protectively round her ribs and a slightly fearful look on her face. "Mom?"

Katie stepped toward Maddie—ready to intervene if things grew more heated.

"Maddie!" Mrs. Klausen rushed to her daughter's side. "What happened? We just got the call that there was an accident."

The tension eased from Katie's face as the anger obviously born of fear for their children turned into protective hugs and kisses.

"Where are your brothers?" Her father pushed her back to arm's length. "I'm going to wring their necks!"

Then again...

"Dr. McGann, I was the one who brought him up to—"

Katie waved Michael to silence. They didn't need to hear the gory details out here with a crowd gathering.

"Sir, perhaps you'd like to follow me?" The last thing the couple's son needed, still in Recovery from surgery, was his father dressed as Santa shouting at him.

"You all right?"

Josh's voice trickled along her spine as she felt him approach. He was doing it again. White

Knighting it in the face of adversity. She was glad he couldn't see her face as she pressed her lips together. Hadn't she just proved she could hurdle her demons in the OR?

Not without Josh by her side.

"Would you like to come with me, Mr. and Mrs. Klausen?" Katie put her hand up in an *I got it* gesture to Josh and snapped a glare back at Jorja, who was busy choking down her own case of the giggles. Most likely born of nerves, but inappropriate all the same.

"What for? Show us where the boys are, Maddie, and we'll get on our way."

"I think it would be best if we had a chat before you saw your boys." Katie was solid now—shifting her gaze from one rosy-cheeked face to the other.

"Maddie…" Josh put a protective arm around the young girl's shoulders. "Why don't we see if we can track down some gingerbread?"

"All right," Mr. Klausen grumbled, his attention fully focused on Katie. "Let's hear how naughty they've been."

Katie led the way into one of the comfortably furnished family rooms the hospital had created for delivering tough news. She and Josh had been led to one like it after the postmortem on their little girl.

No discernible evidence to indicate a problem. Just one of those things.

The words had sat in her heart like an anvil. If there had been a reason, she could have *done* something. Fixed it. Not felt the living, breathing, growing terror that she had no control over what might happen if they tried again.

"So what've they done? How's Eustace?"

"Your donkey is fine, sir." Katie's eyebrows lifted in surprise at the parent's priorities—but you never knew a person's history. Never knew how someone would respond in times of extreme stress.

"One of our surgeons had to give him a few stitches—"

"He was *hurt?*" Mrs. Klausen's hands flew to her mouth in horror. "Eustace!" She exhaled into her cupped hands. "Eustace… We've had him longer than the boys! Our first baby."

Okay. Well, that explained that.

"Your son Chris has some pretty serious injuries. Maybe we should sit down so we can talk through them before I take you through to Recovery."

"Recovery?" Mr. Klausen's face was twisted in incomprehension. "What do you mean?"

"He's really been hurt?" Tears sprang to Mrs. Klausen's eyes.

"Yes." Katie shifted her tone. The Klausens would need a gentle touch now that the fog of displacement was beginning to clear. Rage, anger, even disbelief were common when the worst thing that could happen to someone actually happened. Particularly when it came out of the blue.

"Why don't we all take a seat and I'll talk you through the surgery Chris has had? Then we'll get you up to see him and Nick, who is with him, as soon as possible. No doubt seeing you both will be the perfect medicine."

She hoped no one could see the fingers she crossed in the depths of her lab coat.

Josh eased the locker open with yet another surreptitious over-the-shoulder check that he was alone. Subterfuge hadn't been his initial plan of attack, but it seemed alone time with Katie was going to be hard to come by, so he was going to have to find just the right pocket to tuck his wrapped present into.

He was hit by Katie's scent in an instant. She'd

always smelled like fresh linen with a teasing of vanilla. He gave himself a moment to close his eyes and take a scented trip down memory lane.

A noise further down the corridor jarred him back into action. Winter coat or…? What was that? In the very back of her fastidiously tidy locker, behind the hanging lab coats and winter wear, was a grainy black-and-white printout. The image of their little girl hit him straight in the solar plexus. If kissing Katie on the roof had brought back everything good about their marriage, seeing the last fetal scan they'd had of their baby girl brought back the blackest.

"What are you doing?"

Josh whirled around at the sound of Katie's voice, the sheen of emotion blinding him for just an instant. His hand shot protectively to his hip. He'd turned too sharply. Abrupt turns always gave him a stabbing reminder of how far he'd pushed the envelope. Why Katie had asked him to leave. Why he was here.

To make a smart move. For once.

Katie's eyes flicked from his hip to his eyes. He saw the questions piling up in her deep brown eyes and the flicker of her decision not to ask.

"What are you doing in my locker, Josh?"

He heard the tiniest of wavers in her voice—but her body language told another story. Hands curled into fists on her hips. Mistrust laced through those dark eyes of hers. Her chin tilted slightly, as if daring him to confirm all her worst fears.

He'd gone too far. Just as she'd predicted.

"Even angry, you are the most beautiful woman I've ever seen."

She stepped back, shocked at his words. He was a bit, too, but he meant them. Her face still carried the broad features youth afforded. Full lips. A cute little gap between the two front teeth that had rebelled against the years of expensive orthodontics she'd once confessed to enduring. It made for a slightly crooked smile that lit the world up when she unleashed it. Something she wasn't even *close* to doing now, from the looks of things.

"Josh…" Her smooth forehead crinkled. "Are you all right?"

"I—uh…" He swung his gaze back to her locker, still holding the wrapped package in his hand. The pendulum of Tell or Don't Tell bashed the sides of his brain.

You were right. I should never have taken up motorcycle racing.

You were wrong—you always needed me.

He thrust the tiny package forward so it sat between them like a buffer against all that was going unsaid. "I know it was supposed to be secret, but... Merry Christmas..."

A rush of emotion crossed her face, darkening her eyes so that they were near black.

"I didn't...I don't have anything for you."

"Well, it was the luck of the draw that I got your name in Secret Santa." He hoped the white lie wouldn't come back to haunt him. "It's not exactly as if you were expecting me to turn up in Copper Canyon, now, is it?" He laughed softly, hiding a swipe at his eyes with a scrub along his forehead and a finger-whoosh through his hair.

Her expression softened.

"Are you going to unclench that thing or do you just want me to guess?"

He released his grip and let the small box rest on his palm. His eyes narrowed a bit as he watched her reach out to take it. The paper was crumpled. Worn, even. He'd wrapped that thing up the day after she'd thrown it at him and told him she'd had enough. Waiting...waiting for the perfect moment.

He cleared his throat when her fingers gained purchase on the box, her skin lightly skimming across his. He couldn't even remember how many times he'd imagined this moment. Her response would trigger a chain of events that would either make or break him.

She withdrew the box from his hand. He felt the absence of its weight and her touch instantly. Maybe ignorance *was* bliss. As long as he didn't really know how Katie felt about him, he could believe there was hope. Believe he'd never have to put his signature to that ragged pile of papers he'd been dragging around in the same backpack as the little box she was now slowly unwrapping.

The dawning of recognition wasn't far off. He'd used the same box the rings had come in. Placed them—engagement and wedding—side by side. The rings they had bought with downright giddy smiles wreathing their faces and the last handful of notes and coins they had between them.

There were only two other times when he'd seen her smile as much. Their wedding day and the day they'd found out she was pregnant.

Katie's expression became unreadable. That hurt as much as no reaction. There had once been a time when he could have told anyone her mood before she'd walked into a room. They had been *that* connected. Genuine soulmates.

"Oh…" It came out as a sigh. "Josh…" Beads of

tears weighted her lashes as she held the box open, her eyes fastened to what lay inside. "I can't do this. Not right now. I just can't do this."

She turned on her heel, all but knocking Michael off his feet as he entered the locker room.

"Everything all right?" Michael pulled off his glasses and gave his eyes a rub.

"Yeah, sure." *No*. "She probably just got paged or something."

"Mmm…"

Michael seemed to take his response at face value, which came as a relief. Fatigue hit him like a truck. Heavy and unforgiving.

"Say, Dr. West… Would you like to have a coffee or something later?"

"What? Tonight?"

"No, no. Just before you hit the road again."

"Like a debrief?"

Michael's forehead scrunched. "I guess…"

"Sure thing. Just grab me next time you're free."

He gave him a gentle back-slap as he pushed the door back into the corridor open, smarting at Michael's words. The icing on the cake! So much for his fairy-tale moment when Katie slipped her rings back on her finger and his life became whole again.

He fought the urge to punch the wall. *It* hadn't done anything wrong. *He* had. He'd made a complete hash of giving Katie the rings and now Michael wanted an exit interview. Fan-freakin'-tastic.

His eyes shot up. *More mistletoe.* Merry Christmas, everyone!

CHAPTER SIX

"DR. McGANN, WOULD you mind signing these…? Hey, are you all right?"

Jorja skidded to a halt, openly gawking at Katie. Her go-to neutral face obviously wasn't cooperating tonight.

"Of course," Katie answered briskly. "What can I do for you?"

"Before I go I just need your signature on these release forms for Mr. and Mrs. Wilson."

"The parents of the little girl? The one who had the nephrectomy?"

"Yes, that's the one. Luckily they just had a few cuts and bruises. Nothing serious. So they want to head up to the Pediatric recovery ward. Hey!" Jorja's face split into an impressed grin. "I heard you aced that baby!"

Katie's heart tightened at the choice of words, but she couldn't stop a shy smile in return. She *had* done well. And Josh had been right. She didn't need to be pinned down by her grief. Just needed to learn from it and move on. Eyes forward was a lot healthier than always looking over your shoulder at the past.

She scribbled her signature on the forms and told Jorja where the Wilsons would be able to find their little girl. They must be frantic to be with her. Hold her small little hands. Kiss those soft cheeks of hers.

Katie's fingers tightened round the ring box in her pocket.

"I'm just going for a quick power nap. Are you off for the night?"

"Yup—me and my five thousand relatives are meeting up at Midnight Mass. Spouses, girlfriends, boyfriends, uncles, aunts—you name it. And little ol' me. Late, as usual, and all on my lonesome!"

"There's plenty of time for that." Katie smiled and gave the nurse's arm a squeeze. She was pretty, vivacious, and would be a great catch for the right man. One with lots of energy. Heaven knew, her brothers were busier than an online dating agency trying to find her a beau, if all the staff-room gossip she'd caught was anything to go by. "You have a good time with your family, Jorja."

"You too, Dr. McGann." Jorja's eyes widened as her lips opened into a horrified O. "I mean—keep manning the ship like you always do! It's what you always do, isn't it? Meticulous Dr. McGann!"

Jorja's face contorted into an apologetic wince as she thudded her forehead with the heel of her hand.

"Stop while you're ahead?" Katie suggested.

"I think that's best." Jorja pulled Katie in for an unexpected hug with a whispered "Merry Christmas" before skip-running back down the hall to the main desk, her tinsel scarf trailing behind her like a glittery red boa.

Katie stood and watched her for a moment, slightly envious. Not of her youth—she was only a few years older—but of all that was yet to come for her.

She eased open the door to the residents' room, grateful to see the two beds were empty, and dropped onto one of them with a sigh of relief. Double shifts were never fun—but today had been particularly taxing. Physically and emotionally she'd been through the wringer. Seeing Josh...? That alone was enough to send her into a tailspin. But on Christmas Eve... The night they'd lost their baby girl...

She twisted the small box round and round in her fingers until finally daring to open it again. The night she'd hurled her rings at him... Well...

sensibly placed them on the counter—hurling things had never been her style... That night had been like ripping her own heart out.

She fumbled in her other pocket and pulled out her phone. Yes, it was super-late—but if she knew Alice, there would be no begrudging an after-hours call.

The phone rang a couple of times and Katie grinned, remembering the silly ringtones Alice had kept putting on her phone when she hadn't been looking.

"Hello, angel..." a sleepy Alice answered.

"Hi—sorry. I know it's late, but—"

"It's all right, darlin'. I'm just watching the dying embers of the fire. What's that little scamp done now?" Alice cut to the chase.

"He gave me back my rings."

Katie heard Alice rearrange her position on the sofa, or wherever she was. "What? For good?"

"Well, I presume so." She hadn't got that far yet.

"On bended knee? Or with a scowl in a *Here, let's have done with it* kind of way?"

"Well..." She'd been so annoyed at seeing him in her locker it hadn't even occurred to her that there might have been a plan. "There wasn't a bended knee—but there wasn't a scowl either."

"So," Alice said in her perfunctory Irish way. That meant any number of things, and in this case Katie was guessing it meant *What the hell are you going to do now?*

"I don't want to give them back." The words rushed out before she'd had a chance to edit them.

"In a good way? Or in a *Fine, you've done your business now let me get on with mine* kind of way?"

Katie laughed. She loved this woman. There were incredibly few people she'd let into her heart...well, okay, Alice and Josh were really it... and she'd missed speaking with her.

"I was sorry to cut you off earlier."

Alice didn't wait for Katie to explain herself.

"I know it's a hard day for you, and there was me prattling on about my daughter and all. It was thoughtless. What you both went through, losing Elizabeth like you did...I can't begin to imagine."

"It wasn't thoughtless." And Katie meant it. "It's...it's life. And other people have it."

"What? Are you saying to me you *don't* have your own life?"

Um...a little bit?

"No."

"My goodness. Is that Katie McGann all grown up now? Are you telling me you're done hiding away in your idyllic mountain village, pretending you're the only one to have ever gone through something awful?"

"Say it like it is, why don't you?" Katie muttered.

Alice let her stew for a moment.

She looked down at her hands and realized she'd been fiddling with her rings during the call and had unconsciously slipped them back into their rightful place. On her left hand's ring finger.

"Well?" Alice had never been known for her patience.

"I've not been hiding. I've been…thinking."

"Thinking about getting on with your life or thinking about hiding away there forever?"

"Thinking about letting go."

"Of what, exactly?"

Katie lifted her hand and eyed the rings in the half dark.

"Fear?"

"That's a good way to start the New Year, love." Alice's voice was soft, but then it took an abrupt turn. "But don't go hurtling yourself off of a mountainside with a couple of fairy wings for support."

Katie laughed again.

"I will be sure to have on full reflective gear

and the entire mountain rescue crew on standby if I ever do such a thing."

"That's my girl. Now, let me get some sleep and I'll speak to you soon, all right? I love you."

"I love you, too. Merry Christmas, Alice."

"And to you, angel. And pass on my love to the rascal, won't you?"

Katie nodded and said goodbye. She rolled onto her side, putting her left hand in front of her face, flicking the backs of the rings with her thumb again and again, even though she could see they were right there.

All the emotion she'd been choking back throughout the day abruptly came pouring out of her in barely contained wails of grief. If she was going to let go of fear, she was also going to have to let go of the sorrow that the fear had been protecting. Sorrow over the family she would never have. The child she had only held once. The husband she loved so dearly that the thought of losing him all but crippled her.

She was so consumed with heartache she barely registered the door opening and the arrival of a pair of male legs appearing by her side. She rocked and cried as a pair of familiar arms slipped around her, holding her, soothing her.

Josh.

Of course it was. He knew her better than anyone. Knew she would need him.

After all this time apart, he was finally there for her in the way she had longed for. Present. Still.

He slipped behind her on the bed and gently pulled her into his embrace so that she could curl up in a tight little ball, chin to knees, arms tangled through his, fingers pressing into his shoulder as if her life depended upon it.

There were no whispered placations. No *There, there* or *It'll be all right.* They might love one another, but how could he assure her about a future they would never have? Neither of them knew if anything would be all right...if they'd have the big family they both longed for. If they'd be together at all.

When at long last she was all cried out, Josh eased them down into a seamless spooned embrace. For a moment she thought to fight him. *How could she trust this? This deep, organic comfort she had longed for during those cavernously dark days?* The weight of her fatigue decided for her. She was so tired, and lying there in his arms...the one place she'd always found comfort...she began to feel the release of dreamless sleep overtake her.

It would be all right. Just this once.

It was Christmas.

Her body instinctively snuggled into his. She heard his breath catch as her own steadied. With his arm as a pillow, she became tuned in to his heartbeat, to that warm, spicy scent she would know until the end of time, to his strength. Her own body hummed with a growing heat. A sense of familiarity and comfort.

One night.

There'd be no harm in that. Right? Just one night before they said goodbye forever.

She felt his fingers stroke along her cheek, then slip down along her arm so that their fingers were intertwined. It was what she needed. To simply… *be*. Without hope or expectation. Just some peace. Some sleep. Some long-awaited comfort in her husband's arms.

Josh moved his hand along an upward curve. What the—? He waited another moment until his brain caught up with his hand. It wasn't a pillow he was caressing. It was his wife. And that sweet scent wasn't hospital antiseptic… It was the ever-mesmerizing Essence de Katie.

He nuzzled into her neck, instinctively tipping his chin to drop a kiss onto her shoulder. He stopped himself, then decided just to go for it. It was Christmas Day and Katie was asleep.

His lips sought and found a bit of exposed shoulder in the wide V-neck of her scrubs. Mmm…just as he'd remembered. Silk and honey.

Katie rolled over to face him, eyes still closed, an arm slipping round his waist. He couldn't tell if she was still asleep or not. When they had been together, the night had always found them tangled into one pretzel shape or another. Just so long as they were connected, everything had been all right.

A little sigh escaped her lips and he couldn't resist pressing his own lips to that beautiful mouth of hers.

She responded. Slowly, sleepily at first, but with growing intent as their legs began to tangle together in an organic need to meld into one.

He felt Katie's hand slip onto his hip and under his scrubs. Their kisses deepened. He couldn't believe how good it felt to feel her hands on his bare skin. Especially, he realized with a smile, when the cool silver of her wedding rings intermingled with the warmth of her fingertips.

Her fingers slid along his hip and up his spine,

causing him to jerk back sharply when her fingers hit his scars. She didn't need to know about the accident. Not yet.

"Josh?"

Katie remained where she was but he could feel her heart rate escalating.

"Are those—?"

"It's nothing." *It had been huge.*

"It didn't feel like nothing." Katie's eyes blinked a couple of times before refocusing more acutely on him. He could almost see the wheels whirring in her mind to make sense of what she'd felt.

"Merry Christ— Oh, my gosh, I'm so sorry!"

Josh felt Katie shoot out of bed at the sound of Michael's voice and a blast of light. For a moment he couldn't understand why the intern looked so embarrassed. He was too busy trying to figure out how to explain to Katie what she'd discovered.

"I'll just—leave you to it, then… Uh…" Michael wasn't moving, so why on earth was he—?

Wow. Did twenty-eight-year-old men still blush?

"Merry Christmas, Michael. You're up with the lark."

Katie was tugging her scrubs top down along her hipline. Ah…the slow dawn of recognition began to hit him. No one knew they were married. No one knew Dr. McGann was Katie West. *His* Katie.

"Not really, Dr. McGann. It's nine o'clock."

"What?" Katie shot Josh a horrified look.

He just grinned. He hadn't slept until nine o'clock since… That wasn't a tricky one to figure out.

"My shift started at *seven*. Why didn't you page me?"

"Oh…" Michael began awkwardly. "Jorja said you looked really tired last night, so I left a note with the morning shift to let you sleep in."

Michael nervously shuffled his feet, still unable to connect his gaze to Katie or to Josh, who thought he might as well stand up and be counted.

"Right. I see…"

Katie didn't really seem to know what to do with the information. Or how to explain being discovered in the arms of a man she wasn't meant to know.

"Well, let's get going, shall we?"

"Merry Christmas, Michael," Josh contributed merrily. If he was going to fake it about having been critically injured, he might as well go the whole hog and rustle up some fake Yuletide jolliness.

"Uh… Merry Christmas…"

Katie steered Michael away from the room without a backward glance.

Josh huffed out a mirthless "Ho-ho-ho…" and plunked back down on the bed. *Merry Christmas, indeed.* It shouldn't have come as a surprise. Shouldn't hurt so much. A psychiatrist would have a field day with them. No fluid Seven Stages of Grief for the Wests! No, sir. Just a tangled mess of How-the-Hell-Did-We-End-Up-Like-This?

He scrubbed at his thickly stubbled jaw. It had been a long time since he'd thought of himself as a plural. They had both been bulldozed by shock. At least they'd done *that* by the book. He'd skipped the next few stages and gone straight to testing. Testing limits. Pushing boundaries. Trying his best to show Katie there was still so much life to be lived and all along only succeeding in pushing her away. Making her more fearful than he had ever thought she could be.

From everything he'd seen, she was still sitting pretty in the snowcapped Village of Denial. As long as she didn't see him, everything that had happened could be her own little secret, locked away wherever it was she locked things up.

His heart ached for her, and at the same time he

wanted to roar with fury at how fruitless blocking out the past was.

Hmm...good one. Anger.

Okay. He'd probably hit that one a few times, too. Depression? Didn't really compute. He simply wasn't that kind of guy. There were too many good things in life to counterweight the sorrows. Otherwise—what was the point?

Bargaining?

Maybe that was what being here was. If he won Katie back then his life would feel complete again. Just like in these last few precious hours. The first time he'd held his wife in his arms for two years. The first solid sleep he was guessing either of them had had since the split. The first time he'd let himself really believe they might be together again.

If he didn't believe...?

Nah. He wasn't there yet. No point in accepting things you didn't know the answer to.

"Dr. West! Good of you to finally join us."

Katie was back to her crisp efficient self. Surprise, surprise.

"Granny dump in Four."

She handed him a file without a second look. *Wow. Talk about terse!* Even at her most efficient

Katie was never rude. Her heart normally bled for the elderly people families dropped off in the ER on Christmas Day so they wouldn't have to look after them on the holiday. It happened a lot in the city. Had to be pretty rare out in these parts.

He watched her reorder a few files, the crease between his eyebrows deepening. Katie knew exactly how Josh felt about caring for the elderly, given he had been near enough raised by his grandmother, with his parents so busy on the farm. He clamped his teeth together to bite back a snarky comeback. He'd expected more from her. Maybe she *had* changed and he was the last one to see it. The last one to accept the truth. They were different people now.

He shook his head. This sat wrong. At the very least she should have opted to tell him the condition the so-called "dump" was for.

He glanced at the chart.

"Peripheral edema." The notes went on to say the patient was complaining of swollen ankles and feet. Could be anything. Ankle sprain, obesity, osteoarthritis—and so the list went on, all the way up to congestive heart failure. That would have to be one cold family to drop their grandmother off at the ER, without so much as grandchild in tow.

"And what have *you* got this fine Christmas morn?" Josh asked Katie, thinking he'd make a stab at civility. It wasn't like they'd spent the night wrapped in each other's arms or anything.

"New bride having a panic attack." Her eyes flicked to his. "Trying to live up to unrealistic expectations."

He turned and went to Exam Four. She was obviously in a mood. He'd already opened up about his expectations. She'd felt his scars. Thought the worst. Maybe this was her way of saying all bets were off.

He stopped just before entering his cubicle and turned, catching a glimpse of Katie's hand as she went into the cubicle beside him.

Ha! He just resisted throwing a punch up into the air. She still wore the rings. Hadn't sent him to the scrap heap just yet.

A grin lit up his face. Maybe it *was* going to be a merry Christmas after all.

"Now, Mrs. Hitchins, is it? I'm Dr. West. I understand you're not feeling at your best?"

"I don't think this is working."

The young woman sitting on the exam table lowered the paper bag she'd been breathing into when Katie entered.

"Is she going to be all right? Is she having a heart attack?" asked the young man beside her, presumably her husband. His face was laced with anxiety.

Katie pulled her stethoscope from around her neck and gave the couple as reassuring a smile as she could muster.

"I understand you've got your in-laws visiting for the first time, Mrs. Davis?"

"My family. Yes." Her husband answered for her. "Emily had just put the roast in the oven and then my mother, who has *always* made our Christmas dinners in the past, started asking about what Emily's family ate for Christmas. The next thing I knew, she was hyperventilating, saying she could hardly see… My mother kept offering to take over in the kitchen, and that's when Emily really took a turn. Is she going to be all right?"

Katie took Emily's vitals while he spoke, gently encouraging the twenty-something newlywed to return the paper bag to her mouth, assuring her husband they would do everything they could to help his wife.

She could hear Josh merrily chatting away with the woman next door. He was obviously bringing out the best in her from the sounds of their joined laughter. She would have expected nothing less. He had a wonderful way with grandmothers. Everyone, really. *Why had she been so sharp with him?* He didn't deserve to be sniped at when all he'd done was show her kindness.

What were those scars all about?

She forced herself to tune back in to her patient's husband.

"I'm happy to call my mother and tell her to take over. My mother does a *perfect* Christmas dinner. Doesn't she, Ems?"

Emily's breathing suddenly accelerated, and her eyes dilated as they darted from her husband to Katie.

"Deep breaths, Emily. Keep the bag up. *Deep* breaths. Mr. Davis—do you mind if I have a moment with your wife alone?"

"Are you sure there's nothing—?"

"Absolutely. If you could just take a seat in the waiting room, I'll be with you in a few moments."

After her husband had dropped a nervous kiss on his wife's head and left the cubicle, Emily's breathing changed. Lost its harsh edge. Katie rubbed her hand along Emily's back as she might a small child and kept repeating her mantra.

"Breathe slowly. Deeply. Count to three…count to five…deep and slowly…"

It was what had got her through her first few attacks after she'd left Josh. Part of her had actually been shocked that she'd done it. It had been so out of character! She'd checked into a hotel when her car had all but run out of gas and had just sat at the end of the bed and shaken for who knew how long?

She gave her head a little shake. This wasn't about her. It was about Emily and a mother-in-law whose son seemed to have problems letting go of the apron strings.

"First holiday meal for the in-laws?" Katie asked gently, lowering herself into the seat beside the exam table and making a Christmas-tree doodle on the corner of the chart.

Emily just nodded. Tears springing to her eyes.

Katie tugged a tissue out of the packet she always had in her lab coat and handed it to her.

"Would it be safe to say this is the first time you've ever experienced these symptoms?"

Another nod and a sniffle. A tear skidding down her cheek.

Katie stood and patted the empty space on the examination table. "Mind if I join you?"

Emily shook her head and Katie scooched up onto the table, her feet crossed at the ankles.

"I remember making my first—my *only*—Christmas dinner for my in-laws. I was a wreck!" She laughed softly at the memory. "My husband's family loved their food and they were happy slaves to their long-established Christmas traditions. And, of course, there was Gramma Jam-Jam's unbelievably perfect cooking to contend with. What I *didn't* realize was that most families *don't* buy the entire meal in from a fancy grocery store and heat it up."

She laughed again before going on, pleased to see Emily's breathing was becoming more regular as she spoke.

"I mean, I obviously knew people made Christmas dinner—it was just that my family never had. And when I volunteered to cook for my husband's family, I didn't realize what I'd gotten into until they started sending me emails about how they liked three-peak dinner rolls, whatever they were, homemade cranberry sauce—but only if there was orange zest and no orange pulp— mashed potatoes—but made with a ricer, which made no sense at all. And lots of butter—salted."

She held up her fingers and added another memory. "A big enough turkey so that there'd be enough leftovers for sandwiches to see them through at least the next week. There I was, a grown woman, and I'd never so much as *peeled* a potato, let alone mashed one."

"At least they ate the same thing!" Emily cut in. "David's family don't eat a single thing my family does. Beef instead of turkey, because they feel the one at Thanksgiving is enough. Roasted potatoes instead of mashed. Which is just *wrong*." She reeled off a list of her family's specialties before giving Katie a wide-eyed look. "What's Christmas without turkey and stuffing?" She spread her hands out wide in a *what gives?* gesture. "I mean—I've never, *ever* had Christmas without turkey and stuffing! It's like a sign that this whole marriage was never meant to happen!"

"Hey," Katie soothed. "Marriage involves a whole lot of things we don't think about when we say our vows. But you can *do* this! Think about your guy. Maybe he's been pining for beef each Christmas he's spent with your family? Embrace the changes as learning opportunities. Doesn't mean they have to be *your* things."

She took both of her patient's hands in her own and gave a decisive nod. "How 'bout this? When your in-laws leave, why don't you make a turkey for New Year's? Just the two of you. Stuffing. Mashed potatoes. The whole nine yards."

Emily sniffled, swiping at her tears to reveal a hint of a smile, giving Katie a nod to continue. Not that she would have been able to stop her. She was on a roll now. Her own marriage might be in tatters, but she damn well wasn't going to let *this* pair of young lovers fall to bits over a piece of roast beef!

"Have your *own* traditions! My husband and I made ours. Pancakes on Tuesdays after a double shift. Grilled cheese sandwiches with pickles and tomato soup on Valentine's..."

Katie felt a flush of pleasure begin to color her cheeks at the memory of the goofy traditions they'd made up through the years, then sobered. She was at work here—not on a magical trip down memory lane.

"You know what, Emily? If your mother-in-law is so desperate to cook...let her! Have your husband drive you home via a restaurant and get a to-go bag filled to the brim with turkey sandwiches—then put your feet up and enjoy letting someone else cook dinner. I bet you've spent days making the house and everything just perfect?"

Emily nodded, the light shadows under her eyes

offering the proof that Katie wasn't just making a stab in the dark. "I do feel pretty tired."

"Okay! Why not go home, play the sick card? Put your feet up and enjoy the day with your husband. Play a board game and enjoy the aromas wafting from the kitchen. And in a few days… when they're gone…pull out your apron and make exactly what you want—just for the two of you. It sounds to me like you know how to cook! That's more than *I* could ever do!"

"The grilled cheese sandwiches?" Emily grinned at her.

"Burned at the corners, gooey in the middle. My specialty." Katie smiled back, giving her patient's knee a knowing pat. Family life could be tough. And the holidays could make it tougher.

"Don't give yourself such a hard time, Dr. McGann."

Katie started when Josh poked his head into the exam area, with his own patient grinning up at him adoringly from her wheelchair.

"I have it on good authority that your husband thinks your cooking is fantastic."

He dropped her a wink and pushed Mrs. Hitchins away, leaving Katie at a loss for words.

"He's cute. If your husband is anything like *him*..." Emily gave a low whistle of appreciation.

Katie briskly jumped off the exam table. Her husband was *nothing* like the Josh who'd just strolled past as if they hadn't just spent the past two years apart. This guy seemed reliable, steady...*present*. Someone she could trust *not* to scale sheer cliff faces or zip wire across the Grand Canyon. *That* was the Josh she knew. This guy...? He might have some scars she didn't know anything about...but he was here for her exactly when she needed him and she hadn't even known it.

"So!" Katie picked up Emily's forms. "I'm going to make a note that you were suffering from mild hyperventilation. Effectively you had an in-laws-induced panic attack—but we won't put that down," she added conspiratorially. "It is not un-common this time of year. If you like, you can tell your family it was exhaustion. But you know how to fix it now...right?"

"Step back, take a look at the big picture and re-member I married the guy I love?"

Her words bull's-eyed Katie right in the heart.

She'd never done that. Taken a step back from it all. The grief. The sorrow. She'd never remem-bered to take in the big picture. She'd just pushed

Josh away as hard as she could. Even put a mountain range between them!

Images of her heart soaring over the Rocky Mountains with a goofy pair of fairy wings pinged into her head.

For a smart woman, she was feeling like a first-class ding-a-ling.

How could you hide from what was alive in your heart? Especially if it was love? Had time finally given her the perspective to see the situation for what it had been? Awful, *awful* luck.

"Exactly." Katie forced a smile. "You married the guy you love. Now, get out there and go hunt down some turkey sandwiches!"

Emily gave her a tight hug and all but bounded out of the cubicle, tugging on her jacket as she went to find her husband.

The unexpected flush of emotion at their encounter made Katie pause. *Whoo!* She needed a few extra seconds for private regrouping.

So...if Emily was The Patient of Christmas Past...

Had she been so blinkered about Josh's adrenaline-junkie ways that she'd forgotten to look at the big picture? To look at *him*? He had been grieving, too. Maybe his relentless drive to cheer her had been the same desperation *she'd* been feeling for him to weep with her. Sob his heart out as she'd done, hidden away in the back of her closet so no one could hear her mourn.

There just wasn't any way to prepare for a loss like that, let alone know how to react. Had *she* been the one to react poorly? To lose sight of what was important?

The weight of the realization nearly buckled her knees.

What had she done?

The iron taste of blood in her mouth brought her back to the present. *Hey! Let's just add a self-inflicted bloody lip to the mix.* Precisely the Christmas look she'd been hoping to present to her patients. To Josh.

She needed a Christmas cookie.

Stat.

If she got to the staff room fast enough, there just might be a few left after Jorja's grandmother's annual Christmas bake-fest.

CHAPTER SEVEN

"Someone's got the munchies!"

"Hi, Michael." Katie guiltily swiped some crumbs away from her lips as she swallowed down an unsuspecting gingerbread man's leg. His head and arms had already been snapped off and munched. "Sorry, I was just…"

Just trying to drown my sorrows by massacring a gingerbread cookie?

Not strictly what you wanted your boss to say.

"Don't worry. I've already eaten a dozen. Maybe more."

The unexpected hint of a wicked smile crossed his face and brought out one on her own. She had a soft spot for Michael. Hair always a tousled mess. Ink marks regularly dabbing his cheeks. He'd joined the internship later than most medical graduates, having taken a year out to work with a charity in South America. Methodical. Steady. He was a serious guy. Not to the point of being humorless, but it was nice to see a smile on his face.

"Lucky you—getting Jorja as your Secret Santa."

"Yes! Yes, it was most excellent. A real surprise. Incredibly generous."

And a really effusive thanks for a plate of cookies Jorja hadn't even baked herself.

Katie looked up from her cookie to give Michael a closer look and was surprised to see a hint of color pop onto his cheeks. Did he…? Could he really…? Bouncy, gregarious Jorja? Who wore costumes on any given holiday? Well… Katie had been all but surgically attached to her books at university and Josh-the-Gregarious had certainly brought *her* out of her shell. Maybe Jorja brought out the hidden Romeo in Michael.

Katie felt her beeper buzz and tugged it off her scrubs waistline.

911—suspected cardiac arrest.

Katie didn't bother to wait for Michael's response.

The patient was her father.

"Who does a woman need to call to get a cappuccino in this hospital?"

Josh knew that voice. He knew it very well. And he knew the bottle blonde coiffure that went along with it.

"Mrs. McGann?"

"Josheeee!"

Katie's immaculately turned out mother twirled around on her heels with the style and panache of a nineteen-fifties screen legend, holding her hands out in a wiggly fingered show of delight before planting a big lipsticky kiss on his cheek. Nothing had changed there, then.

"What are you doing here, Mrs. McGann?"

And...why don't you find it strange that I'm here?

"Oh, Josh..."

Sheree McGann placed a perfectly manicured hand on Josh's forearm. She was as touchy-feely as her daughter was reserved. No apples had fallen near *her* tree.

"It's Randall. He's gone and had a blasted angina attack and he didn't have any of his squirty stuff left so we could finish—you know—*business.*"

She raised her eyebrows and smiled when he made the connection.

"Josheeee..." She gave his arm a squeeze. "I would just *murder* for a cappuccino. Any top tips from an insider?"

She dropped him a knowing wink, but before he had a chance to answer, Katie skidded to a halt alongside them. Perfect timing? Or damage control?

"Mom! Is everything all right? Where's Dad?" Katie shot him a wary glance while she waited for a response.

"Katie, darling! You didn't tell us Josh was back in town. *Naughty* girl. It does explain why you've turned down our invitation to stay at the condo whilst we're here. Now, what does a girl have to do to find a barista on Christmas morning?"

"I bet we can rustle something up for you, Sheree."

Katie's blood ran cold, then hot, then cold again.

This isn't happening! This isn't happening. No, no, no, no, no, no. No!

She squeezed her eyes tight shut. Then opened them.

For the love of all the Christmases past and present...please be gone!

She eased one eye open. Nope. They were both still there. Josh and her mother, nattering away like a day hadn't passed since they'd seen each other last. At Elizabeth's funeral. That was the last time they'd all been together. At least her parents had managed to make good on *that* promise.

"Oh, Josh!" Sheree gushed. "It is *so* good to see

you again. I kept telling Katie to stop hiding you away in all of those specialist hospitals and to join us up here in the Canyon. What did she do to finally lure you to our little mountain retreat?"

"Mom!"

Katie blanked Josh's wide-eyed expression. So she hadn't strictly told her parents she and Josh were no longer together? So what? They'd never been close. On top of which, shouldn't her mother be behaving a bit more as if her husband was having a heart attack?

"Where's Dad?" She wheeled on Josh. "Are you—is *someone*—looking after my father? I just got a 911."

"That was me, dear. I wanted to get back home as soon as..."

Her mother's voice trailed off and she pulled back to view her daughter at arm's length.

"Oh, honey. Couldn't you have made a bit more of an effort?" Sheree tsked as she top-to-toe eyeballed Katie with obvious disdain at her choice of scrubs and trainers. "It's *Christmas*."

Katie crinkled her nose and shook off her mother's comment. Typical McGann reaction. Ignore the real problem and focus on something superficial.

Fine.

She obviously wasn't going to get any sense out of her mother, whose breath smelled as though she'd already hit the wet bar. Mimosas or martinis? She leaned in for a sniff. Mimosa. Her eyes flicked to the clock. Eleven-thirty.

Well. It *was* Christmas.

"Where's Dad? Is he okay?"

"Oh, honey. He didn't have a heart attack. He was just behaving like his usual greedy guts self—eating too much foie gras last night—and he's out of his whatchamacallit… Nitro-something-or-other."

"Nitroglycerin?" Katie crinkled her nose. "You didn't tell me Dad was on medication."

Katie's mother gave a tiny shrug and continued speaking as if Katie hadn't said a word. "Remember what a little piggy he is, Josheee? You know, we were both just talking about you, and I said to him—"

"Why don't we all go see him together? I think I overheard Dr. Vessey saying *she* was doing a preliminary check on an angina case in Two."

Josh smoothed over his mother-in-law's ruffled feathers with the promise of a shot of espresso somewhere in the near future in exchange for a few moments with her husband and daughter.

"Oh, your father won't like that. That's why we had the girl at the desk send out the 911. You know him—refused the wheelchair, staggered in like a drunken pirate, insisting on seeing his little girl. He won't be treated by anyone but you, Katie."

"But—" Katie's face was wreathed in confusion.

"You know your father, dear. You always were his favorite."

"I should think so, Mother. I *am* his only child," Katie ground out, looking a little less like a glowering twelve-year-old.

Josh's grin widened. He was enjoying every single second of this. Not the part about his father-in-law staggering into the ER bellowing to see his daughter before his heart gave out…but all of this complicated, messy family stuff? This was a side of the McGann family he'd never known existed. And on top of everything, Katie hadn't told them they weren't together anymore. It was like fifteen Christmases all rolled up into one!

Out of this world. Heart-thumpingly out of this world.

"Shall we?" Katie bit out, clearly displeased with the notion of the proposed family activity.

Josh tucked his mother-in-law's hand into the crook of his arm as Katie stomped off in the lead.

"Temper, temper!" Sheree stage-whispered.

Katie's shoulders stiffened, but they weren't rewarded with the glare Josh was fairly certain would be playing across Katie's face. She could have whipped round and stuck her tongue out at them for all he cared.

Deck the halls with Katie's white lies, tra-la-la-la-la, la-la-la-la!
She's not told her parents she left me, fa-la-la-la-la!
Merry Christmas to me!

Maybe that dream of running off into the sunset hand in hand with his wife hadn't been so silly after all. And…seeing as it was winter…sunset came early this time of year!

Katie unceremoniously yanked back the curtain to her father's cubicle, shooting Josh a *back off, pal* look as she did.

Then again...

"Hi, honey! Will you tell this kid to stop it with her tests, already? I told her my daughter and son-in-law would sort me out. I want Copper Canyon's best."

"I'm a fully qualified intern—" Shannon began,

before her reluctant patient gave her a dismissive pat on the hand.

"They're here now, honey. Thanks for being so attentive. I'm sure you've got a great career ahead of you." He dropped her one of his aging soap star winks in lieu of a wave farewell.

Katie shot an apologetic look at Shannon, indicating that she could leave. She had this one. Josh received a similar look, but it was a bit more of a bug-eyed *Scram, pal!*

"Oh, don't go, son!" Her father held up a hand in protest. "Josh, Katie's mother and I have been asking ourselves why you and Katie haven't come up to the house yet. Heaven knows we've had no luck getting Katie up this season—as per normal. Where's she been hiding you anyway? It's been— has it been *years* since we've laid eyes on you? Sheree, honey—when was the last time we saw Josheee here?"

"Dad! Can you stop jabbering for a minute, please? I just want to listen to your heart."

Katie fastidiously avoided Josh's twinkling blue eyes, blowing a breath or two onto her stethoscope before positioning it over her father's heart.

Randall McGann's words were like music to Josh's ears.

They really don't know. Katie hasn't told them.

He ran the words over and over in his mind like a healing mantra.

A few seconds of silence reigned before Katie's mother jumped in.

"Darling, I think your father just needs a refill of his medicine. This little incident started when we were in the middle of a…a *bedroom workout.*" Mrs. McGann's voice slipped into a slinky-dinky tone appropriate for a perfume commercial and her husband gave a knowing chortle. "If you know what I mean."

"Gross." Katie shook away the mental image building in her head. "Mom. Just… Can we stick with the facts, please?"

"What, honey? Your father and I were having sex. You and Josheee still have sex, right? It's what loving couples do?"

"Mom!" Katie's eyes darted to Josh and then assumed a full glower on her mother. "Can we *please* just…?" Katie huffed out a sigh. "Dad. Can you tell me what sensations you experienced?"

"Well, your mother was in the middle of a new trick she read about in a magazine, and I was just on the brink of having a wonderful—"

"Whoa! Whoa! Still too much detail. Let's just

stick with your heart. The pains in and around your heart."

"Well, I didn't have the shooting pain down the arm that says you're having a heart attack, if that's what you're after, honey."

"Dad!" Katie's exasperation was growing. "I need details. Did you experience shortness of breath? Sweating? Did you lose consciousness—?"

"Uh… Katie, would you like *me* to do the examination?" Josh only just managed to keep the corners of his mouth from twitching into a broad smile. "I think you might be a bit too close to the patient. Your questions are coming out a bit more Guantanamo than—"

"This is *hardly* an interrogation, Josh!" Katie bit back, fastidiously keeping her eyes glued to her stethoscope. "And I am *perfectly* capable of assessing an angina attack, thank you very much!"

"*Honey!* Is that *any* way to speak to your husband on Christmas?"

"Mom, he's not—" Katie froze.

This could be interesting.

Josh quirked an eyebrow. Her parents, for once, were silent. What to do? Break some pretty painful news to Mr. and Mrs. McGann on Christmas

Day or come to his wife's rescue? The wife he really wanted back in his arms.

He held up his hands in mock surrender.

"Confession time! I'm not really supposed to be here."

"Ooh, you old rascal." Randall threw a high five at him from his hospital bed. "Did you fly in special, just to make sure our Katie's Christmas was a bit more naughty than nice?"

"Dad!"

Katie could not have looked more horrified than she did now. Josh couldn't help but laugh. He might be having the best Christmas of his life, but he would put money on the fact this was very likely Katie's worst.

The smile dropped from his lips.

Second worst.

There would never be a Christmas more devastating than the one they'd had three years ago.

"Nope. Sorry. Nothing quite so thrilling. I just meant I'm on shift, and my boss here—" he nodded at Katie "—would probably like me to see some of the patients I hear building up in the waiting room. Lovely to see you both."

Katie exhaled a sigh of relief when Josh left the cubicle.

"Okay, Dad. Will you hush for a moment and let me get through this exam?"

"As long as you promise to bring Josh over for dinner. Tonight."

"I can't tonight—I'm on duty."

"On *Christmas*?"

"Mom! People don't have health problems just during office hours."

"Tone, Katie! Your mother's had a rough morning." Her father gently chastised her. "Tomorrow, then. Or how 'bout New Year's Eve? That'd be fun. See in the New Year together as a family."

Katie looked at him dubiously. Since when did her parents give a monkey's if they did *anything* as a family?

"Surely the hospital doesn't have you working round the clock?" Her mother added to the appeal.

If only she could!

Her father crossed his arms across his chest. "Sheree—get a yes out of our daughter and promise not to cook."

"Honey—we'll get delivery. I know an excellent Korean barbecue here in town. They do the most delicious ginseng pork—"

"New Year's Eve—fine! Okay? I will bring Josh and we will have dinner with you. Now, can you just *hush* for a minute so I can see how clogged up your arteries are?"

Her father, duly chastened, nodded his assent whilst making a *zip it* gesture on his lips.

Case. Closed.

"You can clear the mistletoe poisoning and the burned fingers from the board."

"Both of them?" Katie's eyes widened in surprise but she whooshed the eraser over the names on the whiteboard.

Josh couldn't tell if he'd startled her or if she was amazed he'd seen two patients to her one—albeit particular—patient.

"Yup. The mistletoe-berry-swallower had to revisit the berries, if you know what I mean."

"Induced vomiting with charcoal?" She gave a shiver at his grossed-out face.

"Not quite the lump of coal Santa had in mind—but, yes. We ran an EKG, did some blood and urine tests and apart from discovering that the hallucinatory effects of mistletoe aren't just a myth, and seeing the magic of receiving fluids through an IV, I think he'll be okay. Michael's just signing him out."

"The little girl with the burned fingers?"

"Minor. But each and every finger. Her teenage cousins were having a contest to see how many votive candles they could put out in three seconds. She came first."

"Nothing like the holidays to bring out the best in a family!" Katie intoned, her eyes still solidly on the board.

"Speaking of which—is everything all right with your father?"

Josh thought he'd better test the waters before going in for the proverbial kill. Telling Katie how much he loved her. Inviting her to Paris. Asking her to renew their vows.

"If being blackmailed into having dinner at my parents' on New Year's Eve is your idea of 'all right,' then yes."

"That should be fun for you!"

"Well, you're coming too, so you can wipe that smug look off your face."

"Ah!" His heart gave a satisfying thump. She hadn't called a replacement.

"Is that a good 'Ah!' or a bad one?" She frowned.

His eyes did a quick dart down to her hand. Yup! The rings were still there. His eyes flicked back up to Katie's.

"Your mother's not cooking, is she?"

"No way!" Katie looked horrified at the thought. "I don't think Dad even lets her heat things up for him anymore. He had food poisoning three months ago, from something she insisted she'd had in the oven all day. Turned out she'd only had the light-bulb on, and had put on the grill at the last minute to sear it and cover up the mistake."

"Maisie's on Main?"

Josh had stopped at the local diner on his way to the hospital when he'd arrived in town. Damn good toasted cheese sandwiches. They'd even put in the dill pickles when asked.

"Nope. Korean. Mom's into 'Asian trilogy in-gredients,' whatever those are."

"Aphrodisiacs, I'm guessing."

"Joshua…" Katie's voice was loaded with warning.

"Uh-oh!" He put on a mock dismayed face. "You only ever call me Joshua when I'm in trouble. What did I do?"

Katie maintained a neutral expression on her face, but the tone of her voice spoke volumes. "Don't. Even. Go. There."

"Which 'there'?" He tried to joke. "The embar-rassing fact your parents are still heavily sexed up and you act more like a parent than they ever did?

Or the very interesting news that you haven't told them you've been asking me for a divorce for the past two years?"

"Holy cow!"

Michael popped up from underneath the central reception desk, much to Katie's obvious horror.

"You two are *married*?"

"No!"

"Yes."

Katie's negative response was drowned out by Josh's emphatic affirmation.

"Not that we're telling anyone—are we, Katie?"

"Uh..." Michael's eyes shifted from one to the other, as if he were expecting one or both of them to sprout wings. Or horns. "I'll just leave you two to it, then..." And he promptly bolted from the desk toward the staff room.

"Now look what you've done!" Katie's expression was one of pure dismay.

"What *I've* done? Are you *kidding* me? All I've done is everything you've asked of me for the past three years, Katie."

Whoops. Not quite the love-heals-all-wounds tack he was hoping to take.

"Everything but one!" She furiously obliterated her father's name from the whiteboard.

Josh's heart plummeted to his guts, then re-bounded with a fiery need to lay his cards on the table. Katie didn't need to know he'd almost died. Didn't need to know he was being offered the chance of a lifetime in Paris. Didn't need to know a single one of those things to know if she loved him. But she *did* need to know them if they were to go forward truthfully. With trust.

He steadied his breathing before he began speaking, but the moment the words came out, he knew he should have walked away. Thrown a snowball. Pulled her into his arms under some mistletoe and showed her the other side of his love. Something—*anything*—to temper the vol-canic strength of rage and sorrow he felt at what had happened to them.

"Is that really what you want? You honestly want me to sign those papers? Or do you just like hold-ing it over me so we can both pretend *I* was the one who pushed *you* away after Elizabeth died?"

Josh could have punched himself in the face when he saw the look on her face.

There had been no need to be cruel. It was just that it hurt so *bad*. A physical pain compounded tenfold when he saw the tears spring into Katie's eyes before she turned on her heel and strode away.

It was time. Every pore in his body was rebelling, but the decision he'd needed to make since his arrival had been made.

CHAPTER EIGHT

NOT EVEN A snow angel was going to help dilute the bad mood Katie was in. A good stomp around the corridors of the hospital might do her good. Instill a bit of calm now that... She checked her watch... Nope! Wasn't over yet.

She glanced out the window... A perfectly beautiful white Christmas. If this day would just hurry up and be over, the little gremlins of Christmases Past could just go back to where they came from! She checked her watch again, tapping the surface of the glass as if the hour hand would suddenly leap forward.

Nope! Time didn't really seem to be playing ball today. Not in the slightest.

She kicked her pace up a notch. Including stairwells, she could get in a good three-mile walk. All she needed was to keep her pager from...

Zzzzt! Zzzzzt!

...going off.

She turned her race-walk into a run toward the

surgical recovery ward. Was it the little girl she'd operated on yesterday? Casey Wilson? She offered up silent prayers as she kicked up her pace. Of all the surgeries in her entire career that needed to come out golden… *Please, please, please…*

If she could just block out the fact that she might not have made it through Casey's surgery without the sandy-haired, blue-eyed boy she'd lost her heart to way back in the innocent days of her junior residency…

She swiped at the tears cascading down her cheeks. Try harder. Block harder. *Shut him down.*

She was going to have to. Lives depended upon her ability to focus and to block out the pain that would drive her wild if she let it surface. Block out the need to be held in her husband's arms and have him tell her everything would be okay when she knew it wouldn't be. Couldn't be.

Where had those scars come from?

Run. Work.

Run faster. Work harder.

She reached the recovery ward breathless, more from fear than exertion. Was Casey all right?

"Hey, Dr. McGann." One of the nurses looked up when Katie approached the desk. "Sorry to set off your pager like that. It's just the Wilsons. They wanted to thank you for everything you did for Casey, and no one down in Trauma knew where you were."

"Oh! Good. That's all right." Katie's heart was still thumping away as she registered the nurse's words. "Fine. Good. Um..."

She saw Casey's parents through the glass door of the recovery room their daughter was in. Faces soft with pride and affection. She felt a swell of pride and a stab of loss squeeze all the breath out of her.

She and Josh could have been those parents. That family. Would most likely have been home with their little girl right now instead of haunting the corridors of the hospital, sniping at each other.

She could see it so easily. The three of them gathered round their Christmas tree, decorated with a mix of preschool decorations and generations of hand-me-down ornaments. A fire crackling away and all three of them sitting together in a sea of wrapping paper, gifts and laughter...

"Can you just let them know I stopped by, got their message, but had to dash? Apologies."

"They're just right—" The nurse looked at her strangely as she angled her pencil in the Wilsons' direction.

"Sorry." Katie faked getting another page. "Gotta dash! Give them my best." She threw the words over her shoulder but kept moving. Away from the memories. Away from the pain.

T-minus I don't think I can do this much longer.

Katie rattled through the days and hours on her fingers and clenched them into fists. Didn't matter.

Too many. That was how many more hours she had with Josh.

She swept past the patients' rooms, hoping to find somewhere else to burn off her excess energy before returning to the ER.

"Merry Christmas, Dr. McGann! Can we offer you some eggnog?" A familiar rosy-cheeked woman caught her by the elbow before she flew past another recovery room.

"Mrs. Klausen?" Her eyes widened at the scene playing out before her. "What's going on here?"

A small card table had been set up next to her son Chris's bed, and the other children—Maddie and Nick—were busy hanging up stockings along the curtain rail. Mr. Klausen was poised to start carving an enormous roast turkey.

"Well, we couldn't let Chris be here all alone on the big day, could we?" Mrs. Klausen asked.

Katie scanned the family, each sporting an atrociously jolly Christmas sweater, faces wreathed in smiles. The delicious scent of turkey floated toward her as Mr. Klausen began slicing the large bird. Gone were the recriminations. The threats to wring necks, revenge plans for Eustace's injuries. There were just faces glowing with happiness. An overall sense of contentment that only being together as a family could bring.

"Join us!"

"You shouldn't be all alone on Christmas Day!"

"Eustace sends his love!"

"Can we at least give you a sandwich?"

A sting of guilt at her brisk treatment of her own parents hit her. It deepened as she wove Josh into the equation. She'd all but built a physical wall around herself to distance her from the things— the people—she thought had hurt her most in the wake of Elizabeth's death. But if she came at it from a different angle…?

Her parents and Josh were warriors. Relentless, driven, undeterred warriors. Carrying wave after wave of love with them.

Flawed? Hell, yeah! But who wasn't? She doubted Santa would have a long enough scroll if she were to start cataloging the ways she might have dealt with her grief in better ways. Been a better daughter to parents who clearly weren't the picket-fence type of mom and dad.

A more loving wife.

"Dr. McGann?" Maddie broke into Katie's reverie. "Are you all right?"

"Yes," Katie responded after a moment. "You know…would you mind if I took that turkey sandwich to go?"

"Truce?"

Katie approached Josh, who was doing his best sit-like-a-Buddha on a gurney he'd wheeled into a quiet corner.

"Truce?"

She tried again, her voice sounding more uncertain the second time.

Josh only just stopped himself from making a snarky comment about not knowing they were at war. But if he stopped and counted just how many scars he'd taken on in the past three years—both figurative and literal—maybe they had been. Heaven knew Katie had been nursing her own wounds, and these past two days had done nothing but reopen them.

He shifted across when she turned and pressed her hands against the gurney to hop up alongside him.

"Want some?" Katie offered when she'd settled.

Josh warily eyed the sandwich she waggled within his eyeline. He wouldn't have blamed Katie if she had laced the thing with strychnine, the way he'd spoken to her last.

"A peace offering." Katie held out a triangle of sandwich on the flat of her palm. "C'mon." She nudged him with her knee. "Go halvesies with me. I'll take a bite first, to prove I didn't load it with mistletoe berry sauce!"

He grinned. *Mind reader.*

He angled his head to take a surreptitious look at her through narrowed eyes. When she'd plunked herself down beside him on the gurney, he'd figured minimal eye contact would be the best way to go, but now that she was here…sandwich in hand… She took a smile-sized chomp of the thick sandwich and made a satisfied *"Mmm…"* noise.

He exhaled slowly. No doubt about it. No matter the time, date, place…no matter how angry he was or wasn't…she still took his breath away. If this were the olden days, there would be a kiss on her cheek, a hand slipped round her shoulder or her waist, a cheeky tickle somewhere or other and laughter. By God. He missed the sound of her laugh.

"Truce."

He put out a hand and received half of the turkey sandwich in his palm.

"It's from Santa."

"Really?"

"Sort of," Katie continued, almost shyly. "Remember the Klausens?"

"The 'I'm going to wring their necks when I get my hands on them' Klausens?" Josh held back from taking his first bite.

"The very ones. They're feasting it up on the recovery ward. Mashed potatoes, sweet potatoes, turkey bigger than an emu, stuffing—the whole kit and caboodle!" Katie took another chomp and grinned before her tongue slipped out to swoop up an escaped bit of cranberry sauce.

If this were the olden days, he would have licked that off, then hung around for a bit more lip-lock. He shifted again. For another reason this time.

Sweet dancing reindeer, who made this girl so sexy?

He thought back to this morning's escapade with her parents and felt the corners of his lips twitch before giving in to a full-blown grin. They might be the most surreal parents he'd ever met—but they were a good-looking couple. A good-looking couple who'd created one spectacularly beautiful daughter. A daughter who clearly didn't keep her parents up to date with everything in her life.

"Any chance you want to talk me through why you haven't told your parents we're not—?"

"Nope," she cut in, as if she were dodging questions about ditching school for the afternoon. "Aren't you going to eat that?" Katie popped the rest of her sandwich into her mouth, her fingers automatically reaching toward his untouched triangle.

He took a huge bite, smiling as he chewed, eyes hooked on hers. This was nice. And in the best possible way nice. He slipped his fingers through hers, eyes glued to the snow falling outside the window they were parked across from, not wanting to break the spell. This was more than he had hoped for. Just a few moments to sit and eat a turkey sandwich on Christmas Day with his wife.

He felt a tiny little squeeze from her fingers to his, and out of the corner of his eye he saw Katie lean her head back against the wall and close her eyes, a soft smile playing across her lips. His thumb shifted along her ring finger. His grin widened. Yup. Still there.

He took another bite. It was a helluva sandwich.

"I'm on my pager if you need me. And you know Maisie's number is just on the—"

"Go!" Jorja insisted, her finger pointed firmly at the exit.

Katie obeyed.

The instant she turned the corner outside the ambulance bay, she felt her step become a little bit lighter. She tilted her head back and let a huge snowflake land and melt on her tongue.

It was the first time she'd stepped outside the hospital for four days, and the crisp air gave her an unexpected shot of energy. She needed a little reflection time in advance of New Year's Eve, and seeing as it had crept up on her all of a sudden, she was stealing an hour or two of alone time.

The truce she and Josh had been observing had given her some much-needed time to regroup. And the steady flow of patients had kept them both busy enough not to have to talk about things. Sometimes you needed that.

She stood still for a moment, not wanting to hear the crunching of her boots on the snow, and listened to the perfect wintry silence Copper Canyon did so well.

Maybe "silence" wasn't the best word to describe it. Perhaps…peaceful winter wonderland soundscape? Her eyes scanned the hillside—the trees and houses still twinkling away with all their holiday lights. The wind wasn't strong, but there was the occasional creak and shiver of the evergreens as they rocked back and forth with the soothing cadence of a cradle.

She resumed her journey toward Main Street. The call of one of Maisie's grilled cheese sandwiches had grown too loud to resist. There was only so much hospital canteen food a girl could take, and she wasn't technically due back on shift for a few hours now.

With everything that had happened over the past few days, Katie found herself looking at the picture-perfect town with fresh eyes. She'd always been a big-city girl. Moving out here two years ago had been less by design and more a matter of the most convenient way to put as much distance as possible between herself and Josh as she could.

Now that he was here, she realized how little of it she had actually *seen*. Her parents' condo. Maisie's. That was about it. It was all she had been able to handle. How her mother—who only came out here once or twice a year—knew about a Korean restaurant that did home delivery was beyond her. Had she lost all curiosity about the world around her? Or just needed things to be as straightforward as possible?

Probably the latter. It was as if grief had physically filled her up and rendered her incapable of living in a big city. Too frenetic. Too much to process when she could barely take on board what was happening in her own life. And now...? Now she was getting better. Able to take on a bit more razzle-dazzle in her day.

Ready for Josh?

She opened her arms wide, as if to ask the small town what it thought. *Was* she ready? *Could* she consider life with her husband again? Or was all of this just life's way of wrapping up their marriage in a gentler style?

Her feet picked up the pace, as if leading her to the answer. Within a few minutes she found herself outside Maisie's big picture window, trying to decide whether to laugh or cry. Sitting in her favorite booth was none other than Josh West. She could only see the back of his head. He looked bent in concentration over something. The menu? She doubted it. He walked into a diner and ordered one thing and one thing only.

Maybe that had changed.

She moved toward the door, then hesitated. Something about seeing Josh sitting there felt big. Momentous, even. Magic Eight Ball spooky.

Maybe just a quick walk round the block would help her. If he was still there when she'd done a lap, she'd go in. If not…?

She'd cross that doorway when she came to it.

Josh couldn't believe he'd actually done it. Put his signature on the divorce papers. He'd wanted to see what it looked like. Having his name there in black and white. Well… Black typeface and blue ink from the pen he'd sweet-talked from the waitress. He wondered if she would have handed the thing over if she'd known what he was going to sign.

Just looking at the Petition for Divorce made him wish he hadn't ordered anything to eat. Hadn't pushed his curiosity so far.

Nausea welled deep within him and he sucked down the rest of his ice water to try and rinse the taste away. His head began to shake back and forth. It looked wrong. Both their names on those papers.

It *was* wrong. The best place for these papers was in a shredder or on top of a roaring fire.

The past few days working alongside Katie had been good. Really good. But she had shied away from any heart-to-heart business. Which was fair enough, but he was beginning to feel the strain. Two more days and he needed to call the hospital in Paris with an answer.

"Can I fill you up there, hon?" The waitress reappeared with a jug of water and Josh guiltily stuffed the papers into the inner pocket of his coat. No need to make her complicit in his need to experience everything firsthand.

"Mind if I join you?"

"Katie!" Josh's eyes near enough popped out of his head as his wife appeared behind the comfortably proportioned waitress.

"I see you've found the best grilled cheese in town." She slipped into the booth after making a *may I?* gesture and receiving a mute nod of assent.

"There are other places that serve them?"

"Not with pickles." She smiled, then conceded. "Not really. I can't imagine a Korean grilled cheese sandwich."

"Kimchi and Swiss on rye?"

They laughed, then fell silent. Josh linked his

eyes with his wife's, wishing he could dive into them and find all the answers he needed.

"Are you stalking me?"

Katie screwed up her face in consternation. "No…this just happens to be the only place to get a good sandwich at—" She glanced at her watch. "At seven-thirty at night on the thirtieth of December."

"So you weren't worried I'd left town without signing your papers?" The words came out bitterly. He took another deep swig of ice water, feeling a shot of iceberg zap straight to his temples as he did.

"Oh, Josh." Katie's voice grew heavy with sorrow. "Do we really have to do this?"

He suddenly felt fatigue fill him like cement. *Yeah. We really do.*

"What?" He maintained eye contact. She wasn't going to dodge him now. "You mean talk about why you walked out on me two years ago and why the only contact I've had from you is through a lawyer. Hell, yeah, we've got to talk about it, Katie! That's what adults who love each other do."

Her breath caught, as if she were going to contest him, and a moment passed before a sad smile hinged her lips downward. "Not in my family."

"Well, I'm not your parents. I'm your husband.

And the second you ran off to marry me in Niag-
ara Falls I became your family. Doesn't that count
for anything?"

"Of course it does—*did*—Josh. It's just…" She
shook her head at him, her eyes pleading for him
to stop pressing.

"Just *what*?" He stopped himself just short of
pounding the table with his fist. If he was going
to hand over those papers, he had to know why.

"I just thought it would be easier if I went back to
the way things were before I met you." Her shoulders slumped and she looked away.

Josh's body straightened with a lightning bolt of
undiluted indignation. "What does *that* mean?"

"It means that before I met you I was used to
having no one to rely on. I didn't *need* anyone to
get by."

"Is this because your parents weren't around?"
he asked, already knowing the answer as dawn
began to break in his thick-as-a-coconut husk of
a head.

"Weren't. Aren't. Never will be," she droned,
her fingers methodically folding a napkin into an
ever-diminishing square.

"Why on earth would you have thought that
about *me*?"

"Because you weren't there!"

"Of course I was."

"'I'm going up to the slopes with the guys, Katie-bird.'" She mimicked him. "'Off to the track for a few rounds of speed cycling.' 'Heading up to Maine for the switchbacks.' 'Want to jump on the back of my motorcy—?'"

"Okay, okay." He held up his hands. "I get it." And did he ever? Especially when she got to the motorcycle part.

"And I guess..." She trailed off, her eyes filling with tears as she began micro-squaring another napkin.

"Hey..." He reached across the booth and stroked her cheek with his fingers. "What did you guess?"

"I guess I was scared that if—"

Her voice faltered and Josh took hold of her hand, rubbing the back of it with his thumb. Seeing her like this was torture.

"What were you scared of?"

"Josh!" She tugged her fingers through her hair in despair. "For a doctor, you really are thick as two planks, sometimes. Didn't you *see* it? I was terrified to get pregnant again because if losing one child had pushed you that far away, what would happen if I lost another? Or lost *you* to one of your crazy escapades? I just couldn't bear the thought of losing you, so I made the decision that I thought was best for both of us."

The words flew out as if they were all attached to the other in a long string.

Josh couldn't even speak. It hadn't occurred to him for a New York second that Katie had let him down. If anything, he'd felt he'd let *her* down. He was the one person who had been able to draw her out of her shell, make her laugh like a hyena, smile so broadly movie stars would have envied her…

"You know what, Katiebird?" He drew his finger along her jawline and kept it there when their eyes met. "If brains were leather I wouldn't have enough to saddle a June bug."

He felt her chin quiver. Tears…or a snigger?

"I have no idea what that means." She lifted her tear-beaded lashes to meet his gaze.

"I'm saying I don't have the sense Mother Nature gave a goose!"

"Cute Southern colloquialisms aren't helping to make what you're trying to say any clearer, Joshua West." But Katie giggled as she spoke.

"So you think I'm cute, do you?" He jostled her knee with his under the table.

"Maybe a little bit," she eventually conceded.

"Oh, really? And just how big is this little bit of cuteness you are affording me?"

"Maybe this much?" She allowed a pinch of air to pass between her fingers before closing them tight.

"That's pretty cute, if you ask me. My mama said I grew up on the far end of the ugly stick. Never said which end was which, though…" He picked up Katie's hand and put her fingers in a slightly wider pose. "Now, I don't want to go tootin' my own horn, but wouldn't you say *this* much is a bit more accurate?"

Katie gave him a sidelong glance, then burst into hysterics. His laughter was soon intermingling with hers, and it was only when their guffaws began to die out that she realized the handful of other patrons in the restaurant had been caught up in their chortle-fest as well.

"What are we doing here, Katiebird?"

"Apart from ordering grilled cheese sandwiches?"

"Yes, Katie," he replied good-naturedly. "Apart from that."

"Tying up loose ends?"

He shook his head at the same moment as she

made a face at her own suggestion. It didn't sit right.

"Clearing the air?" he offered.

"Getting our facts straight," she said with a definitive nod, as if the matter were settled.

"Hi, hon—the usual?" The waitress appeared by their table.

"Yes, please, Eileen." Katie smiled up at her.

"You know—we *do* have a Brie and cranberry special on for the holidays."

"No, thank you."

Katie and Josh recoiled and responded as one, much to Eileen's obvious amusement.

"Funny how the only two people I've ever met who like dill pickles in their cheese sandwiches are sitting together." She gave the pair a *go figure* shrug and turned back to the kitchen without waiting for an explanation.

Josh looked over at his wife, saw her cheeks a bit flushed with emotion. It wasn't peculiar at all… They were the only thing she'd known how to cook when they'd met, so they'd eaten them. A lot.

"Have you already eaten?"

He nodded that he had, but didn't move. "Have you ever known me to turn down a chance to steal some of your dinner?"

She grinned and shook her head. He would stick around. Show his wife he was a changed man.

"Well, then. Prepare to defend your pickles!"

"Dr. West—" Michael ran to the door to catch Josh before he went to warm up the pickup. "Are you still good to meet up for that coffee?"

"Absolutely." Josh nodded, yanking up the zip on his snowboarding jacket before he hit the automatic doors. "Is it something we can chat about here at the hospital?"

"Uh, well…" Michael sent an anxious look over his shoulder back to the main reception desk, where Jorja and a couple of the shift nurses were laughing at who knew what. "Maybe not?"

Ding! Girl trouble.

"Got it." Josh put out a hand to fist-bump but Michael just looked confused. He lowered his hand. "I'm out tonight—but maybe sometime tomorrow?"

"Yeah!" Michael's grin widened. "That'd be great. Thanks, Doc." Michael raised his hand, then turned it into a fist, making a sort of weird revolution-style gesture.

"Tomorrow," Josh said with a grin, taking a hit

of cold as the double doors parted to let in a blast of icy air.

He'd need a few minutes to get the truck ready in this weather. Beautiful to look at. A monumental challenge if you weren't where you were supposed to be.

"Are you ready for this?" Katie hauled herself into the truck and slammed the door against the cold wind.

"As I'll ever be."

Katie gave Josh a sidelong glance as he turned down Ol' Bessie's radio.

"It was a whole lot busier today than I thought."

"New Year's Eve!" Josh singsonged. "All the ailments people didn't want to pay heed to on the big day and the day after—and the day after that— building into a mother lode of excess straight up to the point of no return."

"I know," Katie agreed rigorously. "No amount of 'all things in moderation' speeches seem to stop everyone from going overboard on the holidays, and this year was no different!" she finished indignantly. Then she thought a moment.

Except on one front.

It was the first time she'd worked her way through

patient after patient, case after case, and come out the other end feeling a sense of being whole again. Complete. She didn't need to visit Neurology to know what was going on. The wounds she'd thought she'd stitched together hadn't been ripped open when her husband had arrived in Copper Canyon. They had never been fixed in the first place—just hidden away and stuffed in a faraway corner that was too hard to reach. Leaving Josh behind was never going to bring Elizabeth back. Or her old life.

Who knew having Josh here would be more healing than she ever could have imagined it to be?

She couldn't help running her hands along the dashboard. "Check out this old jalopy! Still keeping her pristine, I see."

"Yup. I keep waiting for some movie producer to pull me over and offer me a million dollars to put her in a film, but it still hasn't happened."

She gave a barely contained snort. Ol' Bessie was the one thing in Josh's life he took care of, keeping her immaculate. She shook her head. That wasn't fair. He'd always taken care of her. But after Elizabeth…?

Her rigid belief that he'd gone off the deep end had shifted in the past few days. Maybe pushing life to the extreme had been his way of grieving. His way of trying to help her see the light at the end of the tunnel. She swallowed away the sting of tears and ran her finger along the trim of the red leather bench seats.

"Remember what you said to me on our first date?"

"You can sit here, right next to me." His hand patted the bench seat. Josh needed no time to remember.

"We hadn't even shared a soda or anything together."

"A *soda*?" Josh guffawed. "We weren't *twelve*, Katiebird."

She'd felt twelve. All nerves and jittering expectations of the unknown. But when he'd looked at her...

Mmm...things had started pinging inside of her that she'd never known existed. Sparks, tingles, heated shivers—the whole bag of clichéd responses—each and every one of them feeling utterly fresh and new.

So when they'd discovered they both had some time off, and he'd asked her if she wanted a day out in the countryside, she'd pulled together all her courage and said yes.

Josh had been everything she'd admired in a man and in a doctor. He'd been a year into his residency, having just blasted through his junior residency, and she'd been on the first stint of her rotational internship. He'd had confidence, an infectious laugh, a genuine connection with his patients…and a drawl from somewhere down South that had lit her up like a—she smiled—like the big ball in Times Square on New Year's Eve.

Josh barked a laugh into the cab—with a puff of breath that disappeared shortly after.

"What?"

"You barely even acknowledged me when I held open Ol' Bessie's cherry-red passenger door for you. Me being all gallant and gentlemanly, and your big brown eyes were fixed on the dash, the road, the crazy bright scarlet, orange and yellow blur of the leaves we were flashing past as we left Boston. I thought I might've woken up with the chicken pox or something and not noticed."

He glanced over to see Katie smile at the memory and he patted her leg.

"But three days later you didn't stop talking, did you?"

She shook her head no. It was true. And he was the only thing she'd had eyes for.

She looked across at his hands—one loosely resting on top of the steering wheel, the other holding on at three o'clock. He looked relaxed enough, but she could see his thoughts were about as busy as hers were. On her parents? On the rings she still hadn't managed to take off her finger?

She kept her eyes on his hands, wondering how much the past couple of years had truly changed him. She still hadn't worked up the courage to ask him about those scars. What if what he had been through made him someone she could no longer truly access? That was what it had felt like in that awful dark year. Why would he risk his own life again and again when they'd just lost their tiny precious baby?

Josh would argue that no one changed—they just became more of who they had always been, just a bit smarter about things.

She'd changed. She was sure of it.

Her head tipped against the cool of the window. If she was brave enough to ask, Josh would probably say she hadn't changed—she'd just reverted back to the introvert he'd pulled out of her cocoon that magical first year in Boston. Her butterfly year.

"Are you having an entire conversation in your head again?"

Katie couldn't help but give him a congratulatory laugh. "Got it in one!" Then she surprised herself by chasing it up with a wistful sigh. She'd forgotten the comforting side of having someone know her inside and out.

"Something like that. Remember when—" she started, then hesitated. Memory lane could be a rough road to travel. Especially this time of year.

"The apples?" He shot her a quick look, before refocusing on the road.

How did he do *that?*

"Yes…the apples. What was it—three or four bushels we took down to your grandmother's for canning?"

"I think it was more like five. You were on a high-speed race—dodging all of my clumsy attempts to catch you up in a sexy clinch—so I did the only thing I could!"

"Oh, yeah? And what was that?"

"I had to win you over with my apple-picking prowess!" He dropped her a quick wink, his eyes barely leaving the road as he did.

"Ha!" Katie barked out. "Don't be ridiculous. I didn't know you were trying to kiss me."

"Course you did, Katiebird." His voice was soft now. Gentle. "You were just scared of what would happen once I caught you."

She had been terrified. Her whole life she had always been in control. Of everything. It had been easier that way. Easier to understand why her parents had never been around. Easier to zone in on a high-stakes medical career, knowing she could harness her mind and shape her ability to learn into an aptitude to heal. If she let herself fall for Josh, it would be a whole different ball game. Whole different park. She'd known then that she would never be able to control her heart once she gave it to him. And from the increased hammering she was feeling in her chest, it still held true.

She narrowed her eyes and slid them over to the driver's side of the cab to take in Josh's profile. Her tummy did its usual trip to the acrobatics department. Gold medalists had nothing on her!

All of a sudden she hurt inside. Hurt so much she could actually put a name to it. *Regret.* She regretted making Josh decide between adrenaline fixes or her. Regretted packing her bags and high-tailing it without even scribbling a note to explain. Leaving him to grieve on his own.

She twisted the rings on her finger. She still

hadn't quite managed to put them back in their box. The rings she had accepted with a vow to love Josh until her very last breath.

"I don't think I've ever seen Gramma Jam-Jam look more surprised than when we pulled into the drive." Josh's quiet voice and soft laughter broke into the silence filling the cab.

"What?" Katie exclaimed, tucking a foot under her leg on the bench seat as she turned to face him. "You told me she was expecting us."

"You believed me?"

"Of course I did!" Katie insisted. "People don't just *spontaneously* drive down the Eastern Seaboard to their grandmother's to can and preserve and…"

"Uh-huh?" Josh started nodding, the smile on his face growing. "It's coming to you now, isn't it?"

Little ding-ding-dings of recognition started going off in Katie's head, and her eyes widened as each detail began to slip into a new place. "She set me to peeling and coring all of those apples, saying she needed your signature on something down at the bank in town. It was a Sunday."

"Yes, it was. We couldn't believe you fell for it, what with you being a highfalutin valedictorian and all!"

"*You* were a valedictorian!" Katie protested, fingers digging into the leather seat as Josh took a right turn onto the small lane that brought them up the side of the mountain to her parents' place.

"Doesn't count as much when you're in a class of one hundred in a town that wasn't too much bigger." He reached across and gave her leg a squeeze. "Lucky for me you were too blinded by my good looks to pay any attention."

"Ha! As if!" Katie lied.

"Don't go playing coy with me, Katherine McGann."

He withdrew his hand and Katie immediately slipped her own over the spot on her thigh to keep the warmth in.

"Well…that might've been a little bit true. And when your grandmother assigned someone a task—you did it!"

"That is most definitely the truth! Gramma Jam-Jam was a tough taskmaster!" Josh's laugh ended with a sigh.

"I am really sorry to hear she's passed."

"Yeah…well…" Josh drove on for a while before filling the cab with a big laugh. "Lucky for me she had no problem with white lies if the intent behind them was loving."

"What do you mean?"

"Once you were peeling all those bushels of apples, she and I set off like wildcats, scraping the shelves clean of jars, pie tins and whatever else I needed to bribe my grandmother into helping me win your heart."

"She did that, sure enough."

"She did…?" Josh's voice deepened with emotion. "Or I did?"

"Both of you," Katie answered hastily. Then, "You did." It was the more honest answer. "Of course you did."

Her mobile phone jangled, breaking the weighted atmosphere in two.

"It's my mom. Sorry." She winced apologetically as she pressed the button. "Hi, Mom—what's up?"

Josh couldn't make out what Katie's mother was saying, which didn't much matter as everything rattling round his head was making a big enough racket.

Katie still loved him. His wife still loved him.

Was that enough to bring them back together or had time just been too cruel? Maybe knowing she loved him would be salve enough for him to carry on. Go forward. Let each of them get on with lives that could never be the same if they were together.

"You *forgot*?"

Katie's voice had careened up a few octaves.

"Mom, not even five days have passed since you asked us. How could you forget?"

She listened in silence, then gave a brusque "goodbye" before jabbing a finger at her phone to end the call.

"Typical."

"What?"

"My parents are out tonight."

"Better offer?"

"Something like that."

"Are they in town?"

"They're at someone else's condo in the complex. 'Too good an invitation to refuse.'" Katie expertly mimicked her mother's mid-Atlantic accent, then huffed out an exasperated sigh. "I don't know why I let it get to me. Why I didn't *expect* it! You'd think after thirty-one years of being dodged by my own parents I'd be used to it."

"Is that how you see it?"

"That's how it *is*! Whenever I really needed them to just *be* there—nothing else—there was always an excuse. Always something 'too good to miss' for them to go to."

Her words hit home. He wondered if things

would have been different between them if he'd let Katie go through a phase of wallowing in dirty pajamas, with a sink full of dishes growing God knew what kind of mold. It had killed him to see her so low, and he'd all but turned into a parody of himself to try and cheer her up.

It was also pretty obvious that Katie had learned some less-than-awesome tricks from her parents. Leaving him on his own when he'd begun to run out of false cheer and had needed her most.

His shoulders sagged. She hadn't known. He'd had just as thick a veneer of protectiveness over his emotions as Katie had over her numbness. Grief had rendered them both loners. She hadn't been avoiding him for the past two years out of malice. It had been out of grief.

"They should've had to apply for a license," Katie grumbled.

"What kind of license?"

"A baby license."

"What do you mean?"

"You have to get a dog license, don't you?"

"Yes…"

"Well, there are countless people out there in the world who actually want children and don't get them—and my parents have a child and don't give a flying pig!"

Josh took his eyes off the road, reaching out to put a hand on Katie's leg.

When he felt the front wheels of the truck start to skid, he instantly regretted not giving the road his full attention. Black ice. He resisted putting his foot on the brake. Drove into the skid. Everything the rulebook said.

"Josh!"

He fought the urge to overcorrect. And still the truck slid. He reached out his arm to brace Katie against the crash. She had on her seat belt but she would always be his responsibility. And in the blink of an eye, that lightning flash loss of control ended in an abrupt thud and a jerk as the truck lodged itself into a roadside snowdrift.

"Are you all right?"

They spoke simultaneously.

"Yes. Are you?"

It happened again.

They both laughed, their breath huffing out into the cold cab of the truck in tiny clouds of confirmation that they had both made it. They were okay.

Before he thought better of it, Josh unbuckled

himself and his wife, pulling Katie into his arms, holding her tighter than he ever had. He felt her arms come together round his waist, slipping up along his back and pulling him close. Despite the layers of winter clothes, he could have sworn he felt heat move between the two of them, tightening the bond of connection he had feared was severed.

"That was a bit scary." Katie's muffled voice came from the crook of his neck, where she had nestled.

"It was a bit, wasn't it?" He stroked his hand along her hair, giving in to the desire to weave his fingers through it, enjoying the sensation of silk against skin. "We're all right, Katiebird. We're all right now."

Talk about a loaded statement!

He tugged her in a bit closer, not having a clue *what* they were. Together? Apart? Wrapping things up for good or starting afresh?

Whichever way the wind blew, he would be forever grateful for having her in his arms right now. Feeling her nestle into him a bit more, not pushing him away, hearing their breathing steady a bit. The skid and the jolting snowdrift stop had been a shock. Not a horrible one. But one that needed this sort of quiet recovery time.

He was surprised to discover that his fingers had taken on a will of their own and had shifted beneath the pashmina Katie had tied loosely round her neck. They were slipping up and along her neck, just to the base of her hairline, massaging away any stress or worry. As his awareness of her response to his caresses grew, so did the depth of their breathing. They weren't in their own worlds any longer.

Katie felt Josh spread his fingers wide along her back, fluidly changing the movement into slow circular caresses. Each change of pressure quickened her pulse. The ache of desire overrode her need to intellectualize the moment. She tilted up her chin and after a microscopic hesitation her lips met his.

The explosion of sensation all but overwhelmed her. Heat, scent, taste... Everything was accentuated. Her heartbeat accelerated as the fulfillment from each kiss deepened. Josh's touch felt simultaneously familiar and forbidden. Familiar after the years of shared history. Forbidden because of the deep well of pleasure she felt at his touch. Pleasure she didn't feel she deserved.

As their lips touched and explored, Katie felt as though her body was going through a reawakening. Where she had felt exhausted and dark, she now felt charged and vibrant. Where she had felt deep, weighted sorrow, she now began to feel possibility and renewal. Where she had felt numb... she now felt love.

Her fingers pressed into her husband's shoulders as their breath intermingled in searching kiss after kiss. When it seemed as though time had all but stood still, she felt him pull back. She felt the loss of his embrace instantly and it struck her how time and again over their courtship and marriage Josh had been nothing short of her pillar of strength. Almost shyly, she looked up to meet his blue eyes.

"Look at us, steaming up the windows like a couple of high school kids." Josh's voice was light, but the mood in the truck was laden with meaning. Past, present, future...too much to think about. Too much to consider.

Katie suddenly began to feel claustrophobic in the cab. "We should probably see if we can get the truck out of the drift in case anyone else comes along this road." She pushed open the door, surprised to find it resisting.

"I think we're wedged up against the bank. Come on out my side. We'll have a look."

Josh was reaching across her as he spoke, flicking open the glove compartment, raking around by touch as there had never been a cab light in the old truck. She drew back in the seat, surprised at how Josh's touch suddenly had become something to avoid. Having his warm body all but wrapped around her just moments ago had been like accepting a vital life force, but now that her brain had taken a few moments to play catch-up, she was treating the poor man like he was toxic. It wasn't fair. To either of them.

He tugged a flashlight out of the glove box, clicking the beam off and on as he pulled back into the driver's seat. "Guess that's us in action."

His voice sounded unchanged. Had he not noticed her flinch at his touch, or was he choosing to ignore it—his modus operandi of The Dark Days.

"Can we just get out of here?" Katie knew she sounded impatient, but she didn't have the wherewithal to edit herself. "I feel like a sitting target."

In more ways than one.

"Not a problem." He stepped aside as she clambered out of the truck—a bit less gracefully than she'd intended, but suddenly a deep breath of icy air was paramount. She let the sharpness of the cold hit her lungs hard—hold her static for a moment and then release her with a billow of breath.

"You all right?" Josh's voice was all concern, but

his focus was on the front of the truck—the front half of which was soundly encased in the snow-drift, as if it had been put there before the winter had begun.

She mumbled an affirmative, working her hands round herself and giving her arms a rub as she looked around at the quiet lane, surprised at how much she could see without streetlights. It was snowing lightly. And it was peaceful. So incredibly quiet and *peaceful*.

In any other circumstances it would have been romantic. She silently chided herself. Less than a minute ago it had been romantic! Passionate, even. How could five days have changed how she saw the world? As she thought the words, she knew they were ridiculous. Ten minutes could have an impact. Even less and your life could change forever. For better…or for worse.

She heard Josh crunching through the snow around the truck. "What's the damage?"

"Doesn't seem to be too much wrong with the truck—but I doubt we're going to get out of here without a tow truck. Unless you feel like digging it out of this eight-foot snowbank?"

"Seriously?" *Okay.* Her voice really couldn't

have gone more high-pitched than it just had. Dogs would be howling soon.

"Sorry, Katie." Josh shrugged. "This gingerbread truck has well and truly crumbled."

"I don't know how you do that." Katie shook her head.

"What?"

"Not go mental over Ol' Bessie being near enough totaled."

"Accidents happen. Life goes on." He shrugged it off.

Cool Hand Josh! One of the many reasons why she had married him. Her very own cowboy—calm, cool, and kicking the back tires on his truck.

"Does that make it work faster?"

"Yes," he answered drily, giving the tire another kick just to prove to her that the total opposite was true.

Katie couldn't stop a burst of giggles from burbling forth. His eyes met hers—and the familiar deep punch of connection put her insides through another spin cycle.

Okay, girl—time to decide if we're playing hot or cold. Time to stop playing.

"What are you doing here, Josh?"

"I could ask you just about the same thing,

Katiebird." He leaned against the back of the pickup, one leg crossed over the other—his body language as stress-free as if he were talking about a bowling league.

"I *live* here." Her emotional temperature shot up.

"No, you don't." He tilted his chin up in the classic guy move. "You hide out in your parents' chalet—where, I would put money on it, you haven't done a single thing other than unpack your clothes."

Guilty.

She clamped her lips tight. What *was* this? A standing-up psychoanalysis session?

"When anything approaching life comes to your door, you hide out in your work, just like you've always done."

"No, I don't!"

Wow. Good comeback. Someone has playground patter down to a fine art.

She threw in a glare for good measure.

"Look, Katie. I don't want to fight."

"*I* don't want to fight!" she shouted back. Hmm... Maybe she did. And why not? They were stuck out here in the middle of nowhere, with nothing but a truck stuck in a mammoth snowdrift, and...and... Inspiration hit. She scooped up a handful of snow faster than she'd ever done, crunched it into a ball and threw it at him. It landed on his chest with a satisfying thud.

"Feel better?"

"A little."

She sniffed, thought for a moment about using her sleeve, then sniffed again. Usually she was the one who got to play the grown-up. What was up with this role-reversal thing?

Another little marker went up in her Things-That-Are-Different-About-Josh list.

"Should we get a tow truck out here?"

"I'll call. What road are we on again?" She hadn't been paying attention. She'd been too busy making doe eyes at the man she was meant to have hardened her heart to.

"You're going to laugh."

"I doubt it." Being petulant wasn't making much of an impact on her grinning husband.

"Guess."

"No."

"C'mon, Katie. What do you *think* the road's called?" He drew her name out all slow and Southern-style, as if he were skittering the vowels down the back of her sweater with a revitalizing handful of snow. Verbal retaliation for her juvenile attack?

"I don't know. Rudolph Place?"

"Christmas Lane."

"It is *not*!" she retorted, swiping at the air between them.

"Sure is." He looked at his phone screen, where she could see him increasing the size of their location on his map app. "And if my map-reading is still as good as it was in the Scouts...we've got Christmas Farm up ahead, about a mile. Unsurprisingly, they sell Christmas trees."

"You can tell that from a map?"

He turned the screen so she could see it. A little bubble ad had popped up over the satellite image, with "Christmas Tree Farm" on it and their opening hours.

Ah. So he wasn't all-knowing. Just *mostly* all-knowing.

An image of an admissions form pinged into her mind. "That's where the Klausens live! I thought they'd made that up."

"You doubted the rosy-cheeked and extremely jolly Mr. and Mrs. Klausen's good word?" Josh teased.

"Yes." She scrunched up her face. "But you always knew I was a Scrooge."

"I knew nothing of the kind, my little Katiebird."

She didn't say anything in return. Couldn't. He

knew more about her than anyone in the world. He'd been the only one she had well and truly let in.

"Look—there's a chapel just a couple of hundred yards down the road. We can hang out there. Safer than here in the pitch-black. Have you called a tow truck?"

Katie shook her head and blew on her fingers. "Let me grab my bag. I've got an automobile emergency services card in there."

"Prepared for everything, aren't you, Katie?"

"What's that supposed to mean?" She wheeled on him, handbag swinging around and banging into her hip as she struck a defensive pose.

It wasn't her fault she had had to behave as a grown-up for most of her childhood, let alone after the death of their daughter, when Josh had rediscovered his inner teenager.

"Nothing," Josh replied, fatigue suddenly evident in his voice. "It didn't mean anything. Should we start walking to the chapel while you call them so we don't get cold?"

Katie rang the company, only just managing to keep the bite out of her voice when she discovered they were short-staffed and the wait would be a while. Everyone had bad days. She and Josh were no different. And compared to what they'd been through in the past, this was a doddle.

They crunched along the side of the road in silence, Josh holding no particular path with the beam of his flashlight. It illuminated an icicle-laden tree here. A slushy puddle there. A thickening of the snow in the air all around them. The silence of the snowy night began to close in on Katie. More accurately, the silence between *them*. Between her and the man she had thanked her lucky stars she'd met all those years ago.

Without warning she suddenly flung herself into a snowdrift and began moving her arms and legs as rapidly as she could. She needed a snow angel—and fast.

Josh had been so wrapped up in his own thoughts he'd walked on a few steps before realizing Katie was no longer by his side. When he turned round, he hooted with unchecked laughter. There was his proper-as-they-come wife, looking like a frenzied wild woman. This was going to be the least peaceful snow angel ever created. Snow Tasmanian devil?

Katie abruptly stopped swinging her arms and legs, her eyes locked on Josh so intently it felt like a make-or-break moment. He opened his mouth, then shut it again.

Katie's hand shot out. "Aren't you going to help me up?"

"Of course."

He reached out his arm and felt himself being yanked into the snowdrift. His boot slipped on a skid of snow Katie had smoothed into angel submission and he fell with a thud onto his bad hip.

Containing the howl of pain was impossible.

"Josh!" Katie pushed herself up, a horrified expression playing across her face. "Are you all right?" She began issuing instructions. "Lie back. Breathe steadily. Follow my finger."

He batted away her hand. "I'm fine." He was still hurting and just needed a minute.

"Josh!" Katie's voice broke as her fingers ran along his cheek. "I'm so sorry. I didn't mean to hurt you."

"You didn't."

Yes, she had. But not in the way she thought.

He could be mean right now. Cruel. Because that was what it had felt like when she'd left him. Just about the cruelest thing anyone had done. But he'd known Katie hadn't left to hurt him. She'd done it to save herself. Save herself from a man who'd seemed intent on self-destruction. And here was a sign of that self-destruction for her to bear witness to.

Terrific. Everything going according to the Great Win Back Katie Plan? That's one big fat tick.

He smoothed his hand along his hip and gave it a rub, made sure everything was still in place. Ditto for the knee.

"Help me up?"

"Of course." Katie scrambled to her knees, shifting a shoulder under his to help him up from the snow. "What happened there?"

"Just lost my—" He stopped himself. No more lies. "I had an accident."

He felt Katie tense beneath the weight of his arm, but she just mmm-hmm'd him and waited for him to continue as they both pushed upward.

He took his arm off her shoulders when they were standing and gave himself a little wriggle of a once-over. Head, shoulders, knees and toes all in working order. Haphazard as they were.

He tipped his head in the direction of the chapel. "Shall we get in the warm?"

"Do you need a hand?"

He couldn't tell if she was furious or concerned. Probably both.

He shook his head and they walked on in silence. Josh concentrated on working the kinks out of his hip as Katie visibly struggled with the thousands of questions that were no doubt playing through her mind. She'd begged him again and again not to get hurt. Told him that she didn't have the strength for it. And here he was—giving her evidence that her decision to leave because he was too hell-bent on pushing the envelope had been the right one.

"So…" Katie prompted, unable to wait anymore. "This accident. Was it a bad one?"

"Something like that," he admitted, ignoring her exasperated sigh. "I'll tell you everything you want to know. I just need to sit down for a minute, all right?"

The chapel came into view as they turned the corner. It was a pretty little thing. Clapboard, white as the snow, with a green trim, he thought, though it was difficult to tell in the dark. Twists of fairy lights had been spun round the two evergreens flanking the front door to the chapel, and there was enough snow on the steps to tell him no one had been inside for the past few hours. A large and intricate star was shining at the very top of the church. He would have laid money on it being visible near enough everywhere in the valley.

Katie stepped up onto the entryway first and gave a relieved smile when the door opened. "Thank goodness for small-town security systems."

"I don't know if Gramma Jam-Jam even had keys."

"She had neighbors. Same as keys. Were you...?" Katie hesitated.

He shook his head, knowing where the question was heading. "I wasn't with her. One of my biggest regrets."

A huge mistake not worth making again.

"I'm sorry," Katie said with genuine feeling. "I know how much you loved her."

"Yeah, well...I seem to be chalking up valuable lessons left, right and center these days."

They stood face-to-face, there in the quiet of the church, their eyes saying more to each other than they could ever say aloud. Love. Pain. Regret. Josh could have ticked them off one by one and kept going. He hadn't been joking. All he needed to do now was prove he had learned from those mistakes.

"Let's go light a couple of candles."

"What?"

"C'mon. Over here." He tipped his head toward

the far corner. "Let's go light candles for Gramma and Elizabeth. We've never done that together."

Katie eyed the end of the church where the candle table stood, her head making the tiniest of shakes back and forth.

He wove his fingers through hers. "C'mon, darlin'. Isn't it time we sent our little girl some light—seeing as we're together? Sent her a blessing at Christmas?"

"I don't *want* to say goodbye!" Katie's words all but echoed through the small church.

Josh pulled her into his arms and held her tight. "It's not goodbye, Katie. I didn't say anything about goodbye." He pressed a soft kiss onto her forehead before holding her back at arm's length so he could look at her. "Think of it as her mother and father saying hello. Letting her know we'll always love her."

Katie began to nod her head. Slowly at first, and then in a pronounced yes. She would never, ever in her heart be able to bid her daughter farewell. But hello? She could say that again and again. And yet without Josh she hadn't been able to say anything to her daughter. It hadn't seemed possible. And now here he was—her big ol' country husband—making the hardest thing in the world one of the simplest and most beautiful.

Hand in hand they approached the small table. Josh lit a candle for his grandmother, and then both of them lit Elizabeth's. As the flame flickered and gained purchase, Katie felt an emotional weight shift from her chest—the light of the flame was offering her a lightness of spirit she wouldn't have believed possible.

The moment lengthened and absorbed them both in its glow. Katie tipped her head onto Josh's shoulder and felt his head lightly meet hers. They'd both lost their little girl. It was right that they were doing this together.

As they watched the candle flicker and flit alongside the one meant for the woman who would have been her great-grandmother, Katie could almost picture Gramma Jam-Jam up there in heaven—wherever *that* was—teaching Elizabeth how to make apple pie. As she swiped away a wash of tears, she was astonished to realize there was a soft smile on her lips.

Was this what it took? Being together with Josh again? Josh, who *still* hadn't told her why he had howled like an injured wolf when he fell into the snow.

"Right!" Katie clapped her hands together a bit too loudly. "Shall we take a pew? Hear all about this big bad accident of yours?"

Josh's heart squeezed tight as he heard her trying to lighten the atmosphere. He was surprised she wasn't a fuming ball of I-Told-You-So.

He wandered a few aisles down and chose a pew, patting the space next to him for Katie.

She sat down next to him, but kept her eyes on the front of the church, where garlands were still strung across the apse. A simply but beautifully decorated Christmas tree twinkled away in the half-light.

"It was a motorcycle accident."

Katie sucked in a sharp breath and tightened her jaw. If the light had been better, he would have seen if those were tears that had sprung to her eyes or if it was just the wintry light.

He reached across to take her hand, and though she didn't turn to meet his gaze, he was relieved to feel the soft squeeze of her fingers. He had to keep reminding himself...she cared. She loved him. She might not like him very much—especially right now—but she loved him. It was worth fighting for.

The words began to pour out. "It was meant to

be a Saturday-morning ride. Just a few guys out for a run—before traffic built up."

"But…?"

"But it got competitive. The roads were tricky. In the mountains up north of Boston."

He saw Katie wince. She knew the ones. They'd used to take breaks up there whenever their hectic hospital schedules would allow. When she'd finally taken those first days of maternity leave.

"We were riding the switchbacks and a logging truck came down the center of both lanes. It was veer or—"

He didn't need to paint the full picture. She was an intelligent woman. Move or get mashed was what it had boiled down to. And he'd moved.

"No one else was hurt, so there was that to be thankful for, and one of the guys was an EMT—he made sure I kept my—"

"Kept your what?" Katie whipped round to face him, tears streaming down her cheeks.

He brushed them away with a thumb. "My left leg. It's good. He knew every trick in the book. I hit some dark moments during recovery, and going through airport security is a bit of a bells and whistles affair these days—but I'm all good, Katie. I'm here."

"How long were you in the hospital?"

Josh sucked in a breath as he did the mental arithmetic. "About seven months. Maybe eight."

"ICU?"

"For a lot of it."

"Internal damage?"

"Some."

Katie's fingers flew to her mouth. *Josh could have died.* He could have died and she would have been none the wiser. She'd left no address, no clue as to where to find her. Strict instructions with Alice never to speak of him again. Nothing. For a moment she thought she was going to be sick.

"What happened when you got out?"

"I roomed with a few guys. Doctors. Long enough to know what an idiot I was to let you walk out the door."

"And your motorcycle?" She registered his words, but needed more facts.

"Hung up my helmet, sold the Jet Ski, my snowboard—you name it. I realized life was a bit more important than what I'd been calling living after you left." He laughed. "You'll love this."

Her eyes widened. What exactly would she love about her husband's traumatic motorcycle accident and harrowing recovery?

"I've taken up yoga."

He watched her take in this new slice of information then reshape her face into something a whole lot happier.

"You're going to *yoga class*?"

All right. It was a tone of pure disbelief. But he'd take that over a telling-off for the motorcycle crash any day of the week.

"Three times a week. Sometimes four!"

"In Boston?"

"No, Katie."

He cleared his throat. Spilling this piece of news was going to be almost as rough as telling her about his accident.

"What?" She poked him in the arm. *"What?"*

She poked him harder when his eyes started taking an unnecessary journey round the small church. It was clapboard. There were pews. And a Christmas tree. *C'mon, already!*

"I can tell when you're holding back information. Where have you been? What happened to our—the house?"

"I rented it out."

"What? Why?" She pulled her hand out of his, clasping her two hands together over her heart.

"Are you kidding me?" Now it was Josh's turn to look astonished. "Live there without you? Sit in those rooms knowing the chances of you walking back through the front door were nil to—?" He sought for a word that meant less than nil and threw his hands up in the air instead. "There was no chance of me staying there once you walked out that door, Katie. Absolutely none."

She suddenly missed her nickname. It had rankled when he'd first used it, but now…why wasn't he? *Wasn't she his Katiebird anymore?*

Her stomach churned and she could feel her hands shake even though she was pressing them tightly together.

Was he finishing things between them?

She blinked and stared, her body and mind not comprehending what exactly it was Josh was saying to her. She felt the backs of his fingers shift away a stray lock of hair, then give her cheek a gentle stroke, and she watched his lips as he continued to speak.

"My life was with you, Katiebird, and then you—you left. What else was I meant to do?"

Katie's eyes shifted back up to Josh's and she just stared at him, hands still clasped as if they were the only things holding her thumping heart inside her chest. *She had left him.* She'd thought of it as saving herself, but in doing so had she destroyed Josh? Her eyes took in his beautiful face, the strong shoulder line, the chest she'd used as a pillow more than once.

The pounding in her heart began to drown out what Josh was saying. She could see him speaking, but the words weren't computing.

Okay. Regroup.

Katie ripped through the index cards in her mind to make sense of things. Reorder what she had believed to be true. Reimagine the last two years.

It hit her—almost physically—that what had enabled her to run away was the knowledge that Josh would always be there. In her mind's eye she had vividly kept Josh on the porch of their sweet little house, with its tiny little porch and tinier backyard, where their daughter would be old enough to ride on a swing about now. How they would have got a swing into the backyard was beyond her, but if anyone in the world would go to any lengths to make his little girl happy, it was Josh.

Leaving had been self-preservation for her— but in saving herself had she destroyed Josh? She swallowed. This was going to be so much harder than she'd imagined.

"If you haven't been in Boston, where have you been?"

CHAPTER NINE

JOSH TOOK KATIE'S hand between both of his and tugged it over into his lap, forcing her to scooch in closer to him. Were they going to do this? They were going to *do* this. There would be a serious amount of beans spilled tonight.

They both felt her pager go off at the same time. Mutual looks of dismay passed between them as Katie pulled back and unearthed her pager from beneath the snow coat, the sweater and finally her tank top.

She took a glance at the small screen, then immediately dialed in to the ER. A few "Yup...yup..." then a rattling of satellite coordinates and a "Got it..." later, she stuffed the phone back into her bag.

"We've got to go." Her expression was pure business now.

"Tow truck should be here any minute."

She shook her head. "No. It will take too long and we have to go by helicopter anyhow. Did you notice an open field near where the truck hit? We're going to have to meet it there in five."

"Helicopter? We?" he repeated, as if he hadn't heard either of the words before.

"We are going on a helicopter to help a woman give birth on a gondola."

"A *gondola*? When did Copper Valley become Venice?"

Katie snapped her fingers before tugging up the zipper on her winter coat. "Earth to Josh! The gondolas that go from the ski resort down to Main Street! Copper Canyon's ingenious way to transport its punters to and from the valley has broken and there is a woman in labor. You've got to help her."

"Me?" Now Josh was fully alert.

"Yes," Katie answered perfunctorily, turning toward the door. "I don't do deliveries. Not since..." She skipped over the explanation. "A tree hit the power lines and took out the power for the gondolas. They're trying to get a generator up there, but that could take hours—"

"Wait a minute," he interrupted. "How are you suggesting I get myself up to this gondola if it's dangling somewhere between Copper Peak and the Valley?"

"You'll get winched down."

"No." Josh shook his head. He wasn't being contrary. He just couldn't do it.

"They're short-staffed at the hospital, Josh. You've done a run in Maternity. You did more winchman training than anyone I can call. Who else do you suggest perform the obstetrics on this?"

"You." There wasn't even a hint of a waver in his voice.

"You're stronger than I am."

"And with the metalwork in my hip and leg, I *don't* get winched into airborne gondolas. I'm not up to the gymnastics. *You* are."

"But—!" Katie didn't even know how to finish her protestation. Every rug she'd believed had been cushioning her feet just a few days ago was being ripped out from under her.

"But what, Katie?"

Josh had her full attention now. Medical emergencies were not something she was wishy-washy about, and something wasn't sitting right.

"I haven't been able to do a delivery since—"

There was no need for her to finish the sentence. They both knew what she was talking about.

"Right." He took her hand in his and headed for

the door, already hearing the distant hum of the helicopter on approach. "Today's going to be the day that changes."

Ten minutes later Katie and Josh were watching the ground disappear beneath them as they hustled themselves into flight jumpsuits, secured their helmets and rapidly scanned the small body of the search and rescue helicopter the hospital shared with the emergency services. Bare-bones equipment and no spare staff. It was suck-it-up-and-get-on-with-it o'clock.

Katie had been in the helicopter loads of times over the past year—but tonight everything was blurring. Katie the control freak had...lost control.

"Dr. McGann, we're about four minutes out. How are your headsets working?"

"I can hear you," she confirmed to the young pilot. Jason. His name was Jason. She knew that. She knew *him*. All of this was familiar. Just not the part about going to help a woman give birth in a broken gondola, hanging who knew how many meters in the sky—?

"Dr. West?"

"I'm ready if you are."

Josh's words were meant for the pilot, but Katie could feel his eyes all but lasering through her.

"Jason, what's the word from the crew who are working on the gondola? No chance of getting them down the normal route?"

"'Fraid not, Doc. It's midway between the resort and the valley—right over the Canyon. So we're looking at maybe..." He paused to calculate. "We're looking at a one-thousand-foot drop."

"Three hundred meters...ish. Not too far." Josh's eyes twinkled, making the number seem less horrifying.

His face told a completely different story from the man who had given up speed thrills for yoga. *This* was the sort of rescue he was made for. During their residency he had all but wrestled his way to the roof every time there'd been a helicopter callout. Adrenaline junkie or not—he was the person she was going to have to put all her trust in today.

Tomorrow? There wasn't time to go there.

She let Josh's steadying voice trickle through her headphones and into her heart as he rattled out statistics and tips. It was obvious what he was doing and she wasn't going to stop him. He was pulling out his "Calm Down Katie" arsenal.

"Want to talk through scenarios?"

"A lot of this is dependent upon that door being open, Doc," Jason piped in.

"Isn't there an emergency release inside?" Katie's heart rate spiked again.

"Yes—but I'm not sure they would've figured it out. From the phone calls, they are sounding pretty stressed."

"How long has the mother been in labor?" Josh's voice cut through to the quick of the matter.

"They reckon she started about three, maybe four hours ago?"

"Dilation?" Katie only just stopped herself from cringing as she waited for the answer.

"Not a clue. We're both going into this dark, Dr. McGann. Speaking of which—there are night-vision goggles. You both should put them on."

"What about once we lower Dr. McGann down? How will they work in the snow?"

"Not good." Jason didn't mince his words. "There's a couple of head torches. Better bring those down to work in the gondola."

"Hang on!" interjected Katie. "Aren't we going

to strap her into the stretcher and bring her straight up?"

"All depends upon what you find, my love."

Josh leaned forward, elbows on knees, bright blue eyes glued to hers, his fingers making a lay-them-on-me gesture. She complied, slipping her hands across his broad palms, but part of her wanted to do nothing more than retreat. Trust a man who had pushed life so far he'd nearly died?

His fingers wrapped round hers, heat shifting from his hands up into her body. And then the lightbulb pinged on with full wattage. She loved Josh. Heart and soul. The last few days had re-awakened that knowledge in her beyond any reasonable doubt. But he was the same man who had tested her and tested her when she had been beyond fragile. Did loving him mean putting away her fears from the past and learning to trust again?

"If you look up to your right, you can see the gondola— Wait. I think there are two. That might be the reason for the accident."

Katie and Josh shifted in their seats, craning to see what Jason was describing.

"Is anyone talking to the couple?"

"Someone at the hospital, I think. Want me to patch you in?"

Katie nodded, before remembering she needed to confirm verbally. Josh had shifted across the helicopter floor and started organizing the winch clips.

"What are you doing?"

"Getting you clipped up and ready to go down." Josh dropped her a fortifying wink. "You've got this, my little multitasker. You can listen and clip up at the same time."

And so she did. As her fingers busied themselves with the spring-gated hooks that would secure her rescue kit and the stretcher, she tuned in to the voice of a man describing his wife's labor pains to— Who was that? Jorja? Jorja was on the other end of the line. Good. She was solid.

Katie listened, methodically tugging her straps into place, checking and double-checking the hooks and clips, until she heard the words "I can see something—but I don't think it's the baby's head. Is that all right?"

"It sounds to me as if your baby is in the breech position, Mr. Penton." Jorja confirmed Katie's suspicion.

"We're just about there, Dr. McGann. You ready to go?"

Her eyes met Josh's. Heaven knew what he saw in there. Eight years of shared history? Three years of pain? Whatever it was, it spoke to him deeply. A sheen of emotion misted his eyes for a millisecond, and then just as quickly he was back to business.

"I've got enough fuel to hold here for ten to fifteen. If you think you're going to be any longer, let me know ASAP—so I can get back and refuel."

"Right." Katie put on her medical tunnel vision. Fifteen minutes. Breech birth. In a gondola stuck over a canyon in the dead of winter. Piece of cake.

She looked down at the gondola they were hovering over—high enough not to rock it, low enough to see the door was being jacked open, inch by painstaking inch. She needed to get down there—and fast. If the wind hit and the gondola started to tip—

No. It wasn't worth thinking about.

"Let's do this." Katie nodded to Josh, who set the winch in motion.

Being lowered to the gondola was half-surreal, half-ultra-real. The cold bit at her cheeks, and when she would have expected her heart rate to careen into the stratosphere…it slowed. Everything became a detail—as if she were in a film and watching her own life frame by frame. The silhouette of the mountain. The snowflakes. Her breath condensing on the lip of her winter jacket.

She could hear Jorja offering Mr. Penton reassurances while his wife roared at the hit of another contraction in the background.

It streamlined her focus. If ever there had been a time she needed to give herself a pep talk—this was it. This was what she knew. Medicine. She had this one. Never mind the fact she hadn't assisted in a birth in three years. She'd gone to medical school for over a quarter of her life. This was the stuff legendary dinner party stories were made of! The day Katie West delivered a baby in a gondola!

Josh's voice crackled through the headphones to say Katie was nearly there. A sudden urge overtook her to climb right back up that winching cable and crawl into his arms. Seek the comfort she'd so longed for. She didn't want to do this. Couldn't. *He* was going to have to. She'd just stretcher the poor woman up, they'd winch her quickly into the helicopter and Josh could deliver the baby. He'd always been brilliant with obstetrics. He could be brilliant tonight.

Another female bellow of strength and pain and the sound of impending motherhood filled her headphones.

She couldn't go back up. And yet…

She looked down.

Hmm...vast chasm courtesy of Mother Nature, or get into that gondola and conquer three years' worth of fears?

The winch cable continued lowering her, oblivious to the high-stakes tug-of-war occurring between her heart and her mind, bringing her to a smooth halt opposite the gondola door.

All she had to do was unclip herself and...

Katie lodged a booted foot in the small opening Mr. Penton had managed to cleave with his hands. Three years of fears it was.

"Everything all right in here?"

Nothing like starting off with a bit of small talk when you're hanging outside a gondola!

"Not exactly!" howled his wife from the floor, her hand on her husband's ankle. "Mike, honey, we need to get this baby out of me before I rip your leg off!"

The thirty-something husband threw Katie the pained expression she'd seen on many a father-to-be. Times ten.

He was still straining to hold the doors open the handful of inches he'd managed. Katie braced her knee against the opposite door and took hold of the exterior handle. She wasn't there yet.

"Mrs. Penton? My name is Dr. McGann. You

can call me Katie if you like. Or anything else that suits. But I need to borrow your husband for a few more seconds. We need the door open wide to get me and my gear in. If you could scooch yourself as far away from the door as possible…"

Adrenaline took over. That and eight years of education and a residency that had made her one of the best.

She locked eyes with Mike. "Fast and strong. Let's get these doors open and your baby out. On three—I'm going to push with my foot and you push the opposite door. Okay?"

She counted. They pushed. And with an awkward swing of her kit and the stretcher, Katie got the equipment in—only to have the doors snap shut behind her with her cable still attached. The roar of blood in her ears threatened to overwhelm her. Spots flickered across her eyes. She had maybe six to ten inches of cable between her and the door. The gondola rocked and Katie felt herself tugged and slammed against the glass-fronted door.

Make that zero. And add a bloody nose to the mix.

"I'm going to guess that wasn't meant to happen." Mike's quiet voice was barely audible above his wife's deep pants.

"It's okay." *No, it's not!*

She flicked on her head torch. *Please, please, please let the winch clip be on this side of the door!*

"Get. It. *Out!*"

"Lisa, babe. It's going to be fine. Just push a little harder," Mike coached.

"No!" Katie wrenched her head around, swiping the blood from her face. "Don't push until we see what's going on—all right?"

"What would be *all right* is to be in a warm hospital bed—like *someone* promised me!"

"Well, how did I know they were going to take so long to make the molten chocolate cake *someone else* insisted upon ordering?"

"Whoa!" Katie interjected. "Time for everybody to take a deep breath."

Including me.

"Everything okay down there?"

Josh's voice gave her a shot of Dutch courage.

"In some ways. Others…not so good."

"But our baby's going to be all right, isn't he?" Mike sent her a pleading look as his wife repositioned herself in between contractions.

"I'm really sorry, Lisa, but this is going to take just a little bit longer than you'd like."

"Katie? What's wrong?" Josh obviously had his mind-reading button on high alert.

"Mike. I'm going to need you to pry the doors open again. They're trapping the cable that has me linked to the helicopter."

"What the—?" She tuned out the expletives coming from the pilot's microphone.

"Katie—you have got to get that door open. The winds are picking up and we can't hold her steady."

"Tell me something I *don't* know," she ground out, taking in the fact that her release hook was inches away—on the other side of the door.

"Get this baby *out of me!*"

Short-circuit and potentially kill everyone on the helicopter and the gondola...or get a grip. Those were the options.

"Katie, my love, you can do this."

Josh's voice, soft and steady, trickled through her headphones.

"I'm right here. I'm not going anywhere."

Her decision was made.

"Mike. Your job is to get these doors open again, and I'm going to unclip myself the second you do." Her eyes hooked his. "It's vital we do this now. When I'm free I'm going to help your wife. If you need to use the stretcher to keep the doors pried apart—do it. If you need to rip one of these chairs out to keep them apart—do it. If I can't get to your wife I cannot help your baby. Do you understand?"

"Katie? Have him tie you to a chair before you do anything," Josh directed.

"Grab that rope. Tie me in and tie for yourself as well— *Ow!*" Her face hit the glass again.

"Katie?"

"Fine. I'm fine. Mike's on the case. Aren't you, Mike?"

"For the love of Pete! *Move*, honey!"

Lisa's voice snapped Mike out of his daze, instantly shifting him into a man of strength and action. Ropes were taken from Katie's kit and turned into lassos round the gondola's chairs.

"We've got maybe ten more minutes of fuel, Katie."

"On it. You should have the cable in less than a minute."

"How long do you think it's going to take to get her stretchered?"

"A few minutes."

"I need to push!"

"Don't push, Lisa. *Whoa!*" A rush of freezing air hit Katie's face as Mike yanked open the door, the movement nearly tugging her out of the gondola but for the rope holding her to a chair. She shot a grateful look up to the helicopter holding her husband.

"Just unclipping now, and then I'm going to have a look."

"You're clear?" The pilot hardly waited for the confirmation to leave her lips before peeling off a few hundred meters.

"Right. Lisa—mind if I take a look?" She received a nod as the poor woman tried to control her pain.

"What's it like, Katie? What are you seeing?"

Josh's voice took away the edge of postcrisis that was beginning to creep in now that life-and-death decisions were off the book.

"We've got about eight more minutes of fuel, Katie."

"Can you see my baby?"

For her anyway.

Now that the focus was rightfully on Lisa, Katie could hear fear taking over the roars of the woman's bravura.

"Let's take a look. I can see his— It is a he, right?" Katie received a pair of nods from the parents.

Damn. A tiny baby's buttock was just visible at

the birth canal. A breech birth. At the hospital? Not a problem. Whip her into the ER and give her a C-section. In a freezing-cold gondola, hanging above one of the nation's steepest canyons…

"He's not in the best of positions for a natural birth."

Thank heavens for understatement.

"But everything will be all right, won't it?"

Katie froze. They were the words that had played through her mind again and again when the doctors had first told her they were having trouble finding her daughter's heartbeat.

"Will Huckleberry be all right?"

Huckleberry?

"Don't promise them anything, Katie."

Josh's voice appeared in her head. It was hard to tell if it was real or if she'd summoned up what he might say if he were there.

"Just tell them you will do everything you can."

That's what the doctors had said to her and Josh.

Huckleberry?

Apprehension was replaced by a need to fight the giggles. Inappropriate! *You're a doctor—act like a doctor!*

"What position is she in, Katie?"

Josh was in her headset for real this time.

"We're going to do our best to turn this little guy round."

"That's my girl," Josh encouraged softly. "Are you all right getting the mother into the basket?"

"I need to push!"

Katie began raking through her medical supplies kit. "Fight it, Lisa. Fight it as hard as you can."

"Katie?" The pilot's voice came through as she was tugging on a pair of gloves. "I'm sorry—we're going to have to refuel. I don't think we're going to have enough time."

"I don't think I can hold off much longer..." came Lisa's strained voice.

"Are you kidding me?" Katie demanded.

"I thought you said you could help." Lisa's voice was little more than a whimper now.

"Sorry. I was talking to the pilot." Katie forced herself to speak calmly. "The helicopter needs to go back to Copper Canyon. It means we'll most likely be delivering your baby here and then getting everyone back to the hospital. Mike, can you grab those heat blankets and lay them out on the floor here? We need to get a clean area for Lisa. Keep everyone warm."

"Back as soon as we can. We'll switch to your

cell phone if we lose contact," Josh assured Katie. "I love you, Katiebird. You can do this."

She let Josh's words swirl around her heart as the rest of her body prepared for action. The amount of complications that could stack up against them weren't worth considering. There was only one good outcome here, and the growing fire in Katie's belly told her to start fighting for it.

"I'm going to massage your belly...see if we can shift the baby round."

"Huckleberry," prompted Lisa.

Katie managed a nod. Naming a baby before it came out was dangerous. Naming a baby something that gave your doctor the giggles...? *Awkward!*

"I'm not feeling much of a shift here." She racked her brain to try and remember as many variations as she could.

"I need something for the pain!" Lisa panted. "I had it all planned out. An epidural, some lovely music, soft cozy blankets."

"I've got the music right here, honey. On my phone."

"Why don't you put your playlist on and I'll get you something to see if we can relax the uterus."

Katie's mind went blank as she stared at her medical kit.

"Josh?" She felt like she was speaking to the universe.

"Yeah, babe. I'm here."

Her shoulders dropped an inch in relief. Josh still had her back.

"Talk me through."

"You don't know how to *do* this? I thought you said you were a doctor!"

Mike could not have looked more horrified. Lisa was too busy fighting the onset of another contraction to care.

"You *are* a doctor, and you *can* do this."

Josh's voice came through loud and clear. Katie repeated the words in her head as if she were on automatic pilot.

And Josh continued to speak—a blond-haired, blue-eyed angel in her ear—enabling her to respond, to act, to react. First they worked their way through the basics—blood pressure, heart rate of the baby and the mother, checks for bleeding.

"Do you have an IV of fentanyl in your kit?"

"Yes." Katie reached for the bag, then chose the vial instead. "I think we're going to have to get her on her hands and knees. The massage isn't shifting the baby's position."

"Good thinking."

Josh fell silent while Katie explained to Lisa about the injection of painkiller. It would decrease the likelihood of having to treat her newborn with naloxone for respiratory depression after delivery—but it would need to be given again if the pain increased.

"Right, Lisa, can we have you on your hands and knees, please?"

Mike helped his wife roll to her side and press herself up.

"Good. Now, can you drop down onto your forearms?"

"Why?"

"It's going to elevate your hips above your heart. That's a great way to encourage your baby to shift position on his own."

"Huckleberry, you mean," Lisa pressed as she dropped to her forearms with a huff.

"Yes." It was all Katie could manage. Naming a baby before it was born was too much for her to take on board right now.

"Have a feel and check the heart rate again," Josh instructed after a few moments had passed.

"I think it's working!" Katie couldn't keep the joy from her voice.

"Great. Katie—I think we're going to land in a second. We'll be out of contact for a minute. But I will call you, and you can put me on speaker if you like."

"No, don't worry," Katie answered as the infant inside Lisa's womb turned into a little acrobat. "I think I've got this one."

She tugged off her helmet and poured her entire store of concentration into Lisa and her child. They were going to *do* this. And when they did she was going to turn her life around. Just because the helicopter needed to refuel it didn't mean Josh was leaving her. He'd made it more than clear over the past few days that he had come here for *her*. To see if what they had once shared was worth salvaging. A year ago she might not have been ready. Wouldn't have been able to see the possibility. Now…? Now she wanted that man back in her life, and she was hard-pressed to keep the smile of realization off her lips.

As the medicine began to take effect and the baby shifted position, Lisa called out that another contraction was on the way.

"Great. Good!" Katie responded confidently.

"Mike, do you want to rub your wife's back? Because I think it's time to push."

"Really?"

"Really."

There was a head full of red hair at the entrance to the delivery canal, and in just a few...

"C'mon—you can do it. *Push!*"

And there he was, landing in her hands as if it were any old day. Huckleberry Penton. He was beautiful. Ten fingers, ten toes, a mouth, two ears...as perfect a baby as a family could hope for.

"You've done it, Lisa," Katie said unnecessarily as she cleared away the mucus from the little boy's mouth and nose, making way for a hearty wail. "Turn around real careful now—he's still attached to your umbilical cord."

Katie swiftly gathered together a sterile drape and a heat blanket to swaddle Huckleberry before double-clamping and cutting the umbilical cord between the two clamps. It was cold in the gondola, and the last thing this little one needed was pneumonia.

She dried off his head, resisting the urge to give him a kiss, and handed him to his mother. She kept the swell of emotion she was experiencing at bay by focusing on the postnatal checklist. She gave

Lisa a gentle uterine massage, leaving the rest of the umbilical cord in place and checking that the rest of the placenta did not need to be immediately delivered. It would be safer to do that in the hospital.

"Shall we get an IV into you? It'll help replace all those electrolytes you've been losing and make sure you don't dehydrate."

Tears sprang to her eyes when she lifted her gaze to the couple, saw both sets of eyes wide with wonder, delight. They hadn't heard her. The only thing they could see or hear was their newborn baby boy.

Katie was astonished to realize the tears trickling down her cheeks were happy ones. She was genuinely happy for them. Not that she'd wished anyone ill when she and Josh had lost Elizabeth… but it had been tough to see parents with a newborn. More than tough.

It came to her that this was what she'd been waiting for—the desire to try for another baby. Three years ago she wouldn't have dreamed of getting pregnant again. *Ever.* Two years—she'd become numb to the ache to be a mother. But being with these two—being with her husband…could she really have the strength to try again?

The lights in the gondola suddenly flickered into

life and almost instantly a hum could be heard, accompanied by a slight jerk as the gondola slipped into action.

"Hold on for the ride!" Katie grinned, but the smile instantly slipped from her face when she saw the expressions on the Pentons' faces.

"Um… Dr. McGann…?" Mike began, making a little dabbing gesture with his hand around his nose area. "I think you might need a little cleanup."

Katie's hands flew to her face. Her nose! With everything that had happened she'd completely forgotten her blood-smeared face.

She grabbed for a packet of antibacterial wipes and gently swabbed at her lips and cheeks, happy to note that there was a big grin on her face it would be near impossible to wipe away.

CHAPTER TEN

"Quit pacing."

"I'm not pacing," Josh retorted, feeling about ten to Jorja's twenty-five years as he did so.

He'd been ramped up for going back in the chopper to get Katie down from that blasted gondola, but when the generator had unexpectedly kicked into action they'd been told to stand down. Now he was ready to lay everything on the line. See if it was time to hand over the signed divorce papers and try to find a way to move on or—and here was where it got tricky—see if there were some way—*any* way—he could get the real life he wanted back with his wife.

So sitting down, standing still, anything stationary was not an option. Pacing like a caged beast was a bit more like it. He'd just do it in front of the patient board to make it look a bit more…functional.

"The ambulance should be here any minute," Jorja finally allowed.

"And she's in it?"

Jorja looked at him like he was crazy. "Of *course* the woman who just gave birth in a freakin' gondola on New Year's Eve is in it! What are you? Nuts?"

"I meant Dr. McGann."

"Oh," Jorja replied. Then visibly experienced a hit of understanding. *"Oh!"*

Josh narrowed his eyes. "You've spoken to Michael, haven't you?"

"I work with him—of course I've spoken to him." Her eyes flicked back to the files she had been ignoring.

"About Katie—Dr. McGann..." Josh tried to give her his I'm-Not-Messin' look, failing miserably, from the looks of things.

"Sorry, Dr. West. Nothing's secret for long in a small town. But your business is your business. If you want to spend New Year's Eve trying to convince Copper Canyon's most unavailable doctor to go out with Michael so that *he* can get fired for inappropriate behavior and *you* can get his job—be my guest." She folded her arms defensively across her chest. "And good luck tryin'," she added, quite obviously not meaning the last bit.

Ah. Wrong dog, wrong tree.

If he hadn't been so stressed he would have laughed. He'd have to remember to meet up with Michael for that coffee. He owed him for the red-herring behavior. *Hang on a second!*

"Jorja, are you sweet on Michael?"

"I have no idea what you're talking about," she replied primly, giving a stack of patient files a nice clack on the countertop as she did.

"Jorja and Michael, sitting on a—"

"Dr. West!" Jorja put on her most outraged face. "I'll have you know my brothers are all taller than you." She sized him up quickly, to make sure she'd been correct. "And stronger. I will *not* have my name tarnished in such a way."

"Shame..." Josh leaned against the counter, thoroughly enjoying himself now. "I think you two would make a cute couple."

"You do? I mean..." She quickly dropped her happy face and went for nonchalance. "That's interesting. I've never given it much thought."

"Why don't you ask him out for a coffee? The diner makes a mean cup."

The ambulance crew burst through the double doors, pushing a gurney with Lisa on it, holding her baby tightly in her arms, and her husband by her side, sending a mix of anxious and proud looks at anyone who was looking while the EMT crew hurriedly rattled off handover information to Michael, who had appeared alongside them from the ambulance bay.

Jorja gave her cheeks a quick pinch, even though they didn't need any extra pinking, and flew out from behind her desk with a chart to assist.

They all passed him in a whirlwind of activity, leaving the waiting room entirely empty of people save a weary-looking mother with a pile of knitting well under way as she waited for her skateboarding son to get his leg put in a cast after inventing a whole new style of ice-skating.

No Katie.

Josh looked round the waiting room to see if it would give him an answer.

No dice.

Just the clickety-clack of the mother's knitting needles and the low hum of a television ticking off the New Year's Eve celebrations around the world.

He took a few steps closer to see if… Was that…? *Huh.* Paris. He glanced at his watch. That would have been over hours ago. Ah—there was London. He'd clearly hit the replay… Yes, there was the Statue of Liberty…and cut to Times Square…

New York City was moments away from dropping the gong on the New Year. That gave him a paltry three hours. He'd promised himself he'd have this sorted by midnight. He didn't know if he was Prince Charming or Cinderella in this scenario—but whatever happened, he was going to cross everything he had in the hope that Katie was up for a bit of glass-slipper action.

Katie sank onto the bench in the locker room, relieved to have found the place empty. She'd left the EMTs and Michael to sort out the Pentons and had taken a fast-paced power walk round the hospital, sneaking in at the front door in the hopes of just a few more minutes to regroup before she saw anyone—*c'mon, be honest!*—before she saw Josh again.

If the past few days had been an emotional roller coaster, the last few hours had been… She looked up to the ceiling for some inspiration… *Seismic.* Everything she had held to be true over the past two years had been a fiction. A way of coping with the tremendous loss she and Josh had suffered. But ultimately she had been hiding. And not just from her husband. She'd been hiding from life.

Her right hand sought purchase on her ring finger. It surprised her how much relief she felt at finding the rings still there. Side by side. First one promise and then another. Promises she'd blamed Josh for breaking when maybe all along *she* had been the one who had let him down.

He had changed. She could see that now. But she still wasn't entirely sure what sort of future—if any—he was offering her. He'd said he had come here to Copper Canyon to find her, but to what end? Another chance? Another child?

She opened up her palms and imagined the weight of the newborn she'd just held in them. Tears welled. Could she do it? Maybe she had changed too much. Become too clinical. Or had her time away been more about healing than hiding? Josh's surprise appearance had definitely taught her one thing—there was always room for another way of seeing things.

She glanced at her watch. Three hours and counting. What would this New Year hold in store for her?

She slowly unwound the scarf Josh had twirled round her neck before she'd descended to the gondola, then pushed herself up and opened his locker. His winter coat was hanging on its hook. She folded the scarf and put it in his pocket—but when it was obvious the wool wrap wasn't going to fit, she tugged it out again. A few pieces of paper fell to the floor with the movement.

She knelt to pick them up, eyes widening, stomach churning as she took in the contents of the paperwork.

She shouldn't have looked.

A sour sensation rose from her belly as she absorbed the writing on the letter, the airplane ticket and—her hand flew to her mouth, hoping to stem the cry of despair—the divorce papers.

Signed.

Unsealed.

About to be delivered?

She felt herself going numb. How could she have been such an idiot? Josh was here to give her the signed divorce papers. Why else would he have a job offer and a ticket to France falling out of his pocket? The whole "making peace" thing had just been a ruse to make himself feel better.

Running away again suddenly seemed too exhausting. She pulled her feet up and curled into a tight ball on the bench, no longer interested if anyone saw her. Two years of holding it all together, pretending she was nothing more than a dedicated physician—no personal life, no history, just medicine. And now everything she'd sought to keep under control was unraveling from the inside out.

She lay on the bench, her cheek taking on the imprint of the wooden slats, and for once she just didn't care. Her body was too weighted with the pain of knowing that her life wasn't going to be about suppressing anymore. It was going to be about letting go. She lay perfectly still for she didn't know how long, just thinking. Because once she started to move it would be the start of an entirely new life.

One without the baby she'd had to say goodbye to sooner than anyone should have to. One without the family she'd always dreamed she'd have. A life without Josh. Her sweet, kind, loving husband who had brought out a spark in her she'd never known she'd had.

A surge of energy charged through her, making a lightning-fast transformation into a burning hot poker in her heart. She felt branded. Marked with the painful searing of anger, sorrow and indignation. She'd been such an *idiot* for thinking Josh had changed. It was all she could do not to ball her hands up and try to knock some actual sense into her normally oh-so-logical head. She'd actually believed that he was here to try again—

to start anew. To try to make that family they had both ached for. And…for the most tender of moments…she had believed she could do it.

A primal moaning roar left her throat as she pushed herself up and shook her head. Maybe she could shake out everything that she didn't want to carry into the future. Turn into a whirling dervish and spin everything away. A human centrifuge. It would be hard—and by heavens it would hurt—but she could clear her system of Josh West again. And this time for good.

She glanced at her watch, surprised to see how close to midnight it was.

She needed air. Light. Cold. Anything to remind her that she was vital. Alive. Just one tiny thing to show her that she would survive this.

Josh pushed the plug into the extension cord, not even daring to look for a moment. He knew this was a make-or-break moment. He shifted his chin along his shoulder until he could catch a glimpse of his handiwork. It was cold, but with the wind dying down, the stillness added a strange sensation of otherworldliness to the twinkling lights he'd laced into hearts and trees and stars, to the lengths of decorations he'd stolen from the nurses' lounge.

Perfect. Even if he was a caveman in the home-decor department, he'd done a pretty good job of gussying up Valley Hospital's roof. Now to rustle up something poetic to say about—

He whirled around at the sound of the roof door slamming open.

"Can't a girl get a *single* moment alone?" Katie looked little short of appalled to see him standing there. "What *is* all this?" she snapped.

"Oh, just a little decorating…" Josh started—not altogether certain his words were even being received by his wild-eyed wife.

"All I wanted to do was make a snow angel. One tiny little freakin' snow angel to prove that the world *is* nice, and good things *can* happen, and what do I get instead?"

She didn't wait for him to fill in the answer to what was obviously a rhetorical question.

"*You!* The one person I loved the most in the whole world, leaving me again. And just when I thought we were beginning to repair things."

"Wait! What?" Josh strode up to Katie, hands outstretched in a *What gives?* position. "What are you talking about, Katiebird?"

"Oh, don't Katiebird me." She all but spit at him. Josh had never seen her so riled, and the force of her anger nearly pushed him back. *Nearly.* He ground his feet in and pressed himself up to his full height.

Tough. It was less than an hour to midnight and he was damned if he was going to hit the New Year without finding out if he had a future with his wife. Her face told him everything he'd feared—but he wasn't going to let go of this one without a fight.

He held his ground. "What exactly are you talking about?"

"I'm talking about the divorce papers."

He raised his eyebrows. "You mean the ones you've been sending me by special delivery for the past two years?"

"I mean the signed ones in your locker."

Her stance was defiant but he could see the hurt in her eyes. He wished he'd never put a pen to those damn things. It was the type of thing a trip to the stationery store could never fix. That type of ink was indelible.

His voice softened. This wasn't going remotely the way he'd hoped, but at least it was as painful for her as it had been for him to see his name on those pages. "I thought it was what you wanted."

"I did too," she said after a moment, her booted foot digging a sizable divot in the snow.

"And now?"

"Now it looks like what I think doesn't matter." A guilty frown tugged her lips downward at his raised eyebrows. "I found the job offer and the ticket to Paris. The one-way ticket."

"Oh, you did, did you?" Josh found himself needing to suppress the grin splitting his face in two.

"Yes. Or should I say *oui*?" Katie couldn't meet Josh's eyes but she kept on talking. "Looks like you've gone and done what I haven't been able to do."

"And what's that, then?"

Josh took a step closer.

Katie put her arm between them.

"You've been able to move on. Get past everything we've been through." She lifted her gaze to finally meet his, her tears only just resting on her lids. They'd spill any second now. She tipped her head back to buy herself a few more moments of dignity, if that was what you could call standing on the roof of your place of work and hollering at your husband—ex-husband—for doing exactly what you'd asked him to do.

"When you were busy rifling through my things—"

"I wasn't rifling. I was—" She stopped to search

for a less invidious word than "rifling," accidentally biting the inside of her cheek in the process.

"Uh-huh? What *were* you doing?"

The twinkle in Josh's eyes stirred something within her. She knew what it was, but it was embarrassing to admit it considering the turn of events.

Lust. She just wanted to rip his clothes off and have her wicked way with him.

Would that *ever* go away? She stared at him, her body itching to stomp her feet or jump up and down. Anything to stop the skittering of goose bumps working their way across her body. Wow, did she *ever* need to make a snow angel!

She shifted her eyes up to the heavens. How the heck was she going to carry on with her life when she still fancied the pants off her husband?

"Did you happen to see the ticket beneath the ticket?"

"Um…what was that?"

Best not to appear too keen to have gotten the wrong end of the stick.

"Katie McGann." Josh stepped forward and took both her hands in his. His blue eyes were like sunshine, and a halo of twinkly lights lit him up from behind.

Oh, no, no, no, no... This can't be goodbye. Is this really goodbye?

"I came back here to do one thing and one thing only."

She couldn't speak. The other side of her cheek was being chomped on. Hard enough to draw blood.

"I came back here," he said in his soft, beautiful drawl, "with the sole intent of seeing if you would consider becoming Katie West again."

She blinked a snowflake out of her eyelashes. The rest of her body was frozen in place.

"Katie?"

"Yes?" Her insides had started doing a June-bug dance. Her outsides still weren't up to much more than providing a landing zone for the supersized snowflakes.

"I am presuming you heard what I just said."

A little furrow was beginning to form between the one pair of eyes that could light up a room. What made them so *bright*?

"Yes, I did," she managed to croak out.

"And are you planning on drawing out the torture, or are you going to tell me what you think of the idea?"

"What? About Paris? That job offer sounds

pretty amazing. Groundbreaking surgical techniques? Champagne? I bet it's practically free over there. And the architecture! The Eiffel Tower versus Main Street and grilled cheese sandwiches?" She squawked out a mysterious sound that was meant to say *No-Brainer*, wondering why on earth she was trying to talk him out of staying when all she wanted was to tip back her head and scream *Yes! A thousand times yes!*

Josh rocked back on his heels and gave her comments some thought. Katie's stomach began to lurch as her heart plummeted.

Why had she opened her big mouth?

"A chance to work with the world's best prenatal surgeon? It's a once-in-a-lifetime offer," he admitted, before a near-wistful look added a glint to his eyes. "And I *do* love those baguettes. Especially when they're all crunchy on the outside and that gooey cheese they have is just dripping out over the edges."

"You've already *been* there?" Katie's dog-whistle voice sprang into the stratosphere, her game face all but disappearing as she spoke.

"How else do you think I got the offer?" He thumbed away another snowflake. "But then I got to thinking. Do I sign those damn divorce papers you've been sending me, move on—or do I try to win back my girl?"

Katie swiped at a couple of snowflakes that were tickling her nose, too heartbroken to speak. He'd signed the papers and he had a ticket to Paris. Why did he have to be so *nice* about it all? Where was the adrenaline junkie she'd hardened her heart to?

"All of which is a really long-winded way of saying—" he paused to run the backs of his fingers across her cheeks before tucking her hair behind her ears "—there are *two* tickets to Paris in my locker."

Her heart gave a particularly large thump.

"I'm guessing you didn't see the second one."

"That would be a fair guess." Her voice broke with relief. Josh wanted to be with her. He wanted to start again!

The questions began tumbling out in a torrent. Would this really be a new beginning or would they fall into old patterns? Had he really thought through where he wanted to be, what he wanted to do?

She sucked in a breath, closed her eyes and asked the one that scared her the most. "Do you want to try for another baby?"

She felt his breath upon her lips as he spoke. "More than anything in the world."

Their foreheads tipped together and her breath intertwined with his. "Even if it's the scariest thing in the whole wide world?"

"Even if it's the scariest thing in the universe." He pressed a soft kiss onto her lips. "And I promise to be by your side every step of the way."

"Here in Copper Canyon?"

"Wherever you like." He started pressing kisses onto each of her cheeks, her eyelids, the tip of her nose. "We *do* have two tickets to Paris if you'd like to go check it out."

Her eyes flicked open. A penny dropped. "Joshua West—you aren't chicken to go to Paris all on your lonesome, are you?"

"Ha!" A cloud of breath hid milliseconds of acknowledgment. "As if. But it would be much easier to go into the big new world of surgery with my brave and talented wife by my side. If she's interested in giving up her job here at Valley Hospital, that is, for one in Paris…"

"Oh… I don't know. The boss here is pretty hard-core."

Josh grinned broadly. "I hear she has a heart of gold."

He dipped his head to kiss his wife again. It was a kiss filled with the deep satisfaction of a man who had found his way in the world again. Katie returned each and every one of his kisses with all her love. As they sought and answered each other's caresses, they pulled back for a second to grin when the church bell began to toll midnight.

Katie's heart felt full to bursting. Everything was going to get better now—the healing had begun and the New Year couldn't start at a better time or in a better place…right here in her husband's arms.

EPILOGUE

"Did you get to the bakery?"

"Hello to you, too, my little Katiebird." Josh paused to drop a kiss onto his wife's forehead. "And, *excusez-moi*, but I think what you were trying to say was did I get to *la patisserie*."

Katie couldn't help but laugh at her husband's exaggerated French accent. Tennessee meets Paris was an interesting combo. Not that *her* accent was all that hot. Just mastering the medical vocabulary had been enough of a challenge. But they had both impressed not only themselves but their new colleagues as well. Sure, they both might sound like yahoos from America—but nearly a year in Paris had changed everything.

"I thought I'd go for something different, seeing as it's the holiday season."

"And Emmy's birthday," Katie added, as if either of them needed reminding.

Together they turned to beam at their daughter, her face covered in spaghetti sauce after Katie's unsuccessful attempt to get some of her dinner inside the cheeky nine-month-old. With a head of jet-black curls and a pair of bright blue eyes, she was a reflection of the pair of them.

"So?" Katie prodded. "What'd you get?"

Josh pulled out a box from behind his back. A box that wasn't nearly big enough for the kind of birthday cake she'd had in mind.

"What's that?"

"Not what you had in mind for our cherished daughter's birthday?"

She resisted sticking out her lower lip in a pout. *Just.* "Depends… Is this one of those 'good things come in small packages' deals?"

"In a way…" Josh held up the small box and waggled it in front of his wife's eyes. This was fun.

Who was he kidding? There hadn't been a moment in the past year when the smile had been wiped off his face. The world's longest honeymoon, he had billed it. And a move to Paris. His wife back by his side. A daughter to crow over whenever he wasn't learning about mind-blowing surgical techniques with his new mentor.

"Want to open it?" He held up the package when Katie snatched at it.

"You know I do—I need cake!"

"Need or want?" he teased.

"Both."

He handed the box over, watching with bated breath as Katie ripped it open with the glee of a five-year-old.

The myriad of expressions playing across her face as she took in the contents of the box only broadened his grin.

"This is a napkin from Rooney's..." Her big brown eyes met his.

"Best chocolate cake in Copper Canyon," they recited in unison.

"Um..." Katie looked up at him quizzically. "I hate to point out the obvious, but there isn't any cake *in* here, buster."

"What's below the napkin?"

"Oh, my gosh..." Katie's cheeks pinked as she lifted the tickets out of the box. "Are we *really*?"

"I think the first place our baby girl should make a snow angel is in Copper Canyon. Don't you?"

Katie rose up on her tiptoes and gave Josh an appreciatively lingering kiss.

"I couldn't agree more, my love. Christmas in Paris and New Year in Copper Canyon. Doesn't get much better than that, does it?"

"So long as I have the two of you, Katiebird, I

have everything I need." He gave her another kiss and dropped a wink in their daughter's direction. "But some of Rooney's finest chocolate fudge for our daughter will be the icing on the cake."

* * * * *

If you missed the first story in the
CHRISTMAS EVE MAGIC *duet check out*

THEIR FIRST FAMILY CHRISTMAS
by Alison Roberts

And if you enjoyed this story, check out these other great reads from Annie O'Neil

ONE NIGHT, TWIN CONSEQUENCES
LONDON'S MOST ELIGIBLE DOCTOR
ONE NIGHT...WITH HER BOSS
DOCTOR...TO DUCHESS?

All available now!